VOYAGE
TO THE
STARS

Written by

Richard B. Bliss, Ed.D.
Director of Curriculum Development,
Professor of Science Education
Institute for Creation Research

Voyage to the Stars

First Edition 1991

Copyright © 1991
Revised 1996

Library of Congress Catalog Card Number 91-070369
ISBN 0-932766-21-8

Cataloging in Publication Data
Bliss, Richard Burt, 1923-1994
Voyage to the Stars

Printed in the United States of America

ACKNOWLEDGMENTS

My deep appreciation goes out to the many home school parents and Christian school teachers who encouraged me to begin a "voyage" series in science for their children.

A book like this with its technical implications could never be written properly without consulting science specialists. In this respect, I give my deepest appreciation to my colleagues here at the Institute for Creation Research, Dr. Donald DeYoung, physicist and astronomy professor at Grace College, Winona Lake, Indiana, and Mr. Tom Henderson, NASA space engineer.

Last, but certainly not least, my heartfelt appreciation goes to personal friends who trusted me to complete this book. It is to these friends that I give the credit for creating the seed money that will perpetuate the "voyage" series for years to come.

Sincerely,

Technical Advisor
Danny Falkner, PhD (Astronomy)

Cover Design
Ramona Jeske

Technical Illustrations
Ramona Jeske and Ron Hight

Character Illustrations
Sandy Thornton

Layout and Design
Sandy Thornton and Ron Hight

Proof and Editing
Connie Horn

FOREWORD

by Col. James Irwin

Voyage to the Stars is a modern-day adventure story. The fictional adventure of two young science students studying the stars from the space shuttle perhaps reflects the dream of most young people today, and it may indeed be within the realm of possibility. Even more exciting is the possibility of an *actual* voyage to the stars themselves.

This hit home to me when my good friend and fellow astronaut, John Young, the ninth man who landed on the moon, returned from a space shuttle flight. He declared upon landing: "We are on our way to the stars!" Yes, this was his dream, but this is the kind of dream that makes fiction turn into reality. In fact, this is the kind of dream that ultimately landed me on the moon. Good science, properly taught and learned, will make such dreams come true.

Thanks to Dr. Richard Bliss and the Institute for Creation Research, we are beginning to see good science content with God as the centerpiece. Voyage to the Stars is not only an interesting story about the

Astronaut Irwin salutes flag at Apollo 15 Hadley-Apennine landing site.

stars, but it carries with it some very powerful science content. You will not only reflect on the majesty of God in these pages, but you will learn a lot about science.

Yes, we may be on the way to the stars someday, but the most important question is whether we are on our way to heaven. We need to know God and what he has in store for us. We are here to serve him. I wish you success in your adventure. Reach for your dreams. Aim high. Aim for heaven.

Col. Jim Irwin
NASA Astronaut

TABLE OF CONTENTS

OUR SPACE TEAM

Jonathan Andrew is a senior in high school from Whitefish Bay, Wisconsin. He is a straight "A" student, and has just won the national biophysics award. Jonathan wants to be an astronaut scientist.

Richard Brock is the 1st officer on board the space shuttle, and was also a test pilot for the Northway Aviation Corporation. He has been an astronaut for the past five years with NASA, as well as being an experienced space traveler.

Ann Jackson is a straight "A" student and a senior in high school from San Diego, California. She wants to go to medical school, and would be interested in astro-medicine as a specialty when she becomes a doctor.

Major Steven Paul was a test pilot for several aeronautical firms before he came to NASA. He also has a degree in physics and chemistry from MIT.

Newton is named after the famous creation scientist, Isaac Newton. He appears from time to time in the pages of our book. Although he never interrupts Captain Venture, Ann, or Jonathan, he does give a more detailed understanding of scientific and sometimes Biblical points that are discussed by our adventurers.

INTRODUCTION & PURPOSE

Our scientist, Captain Venture, has a very distinguished background as a captain in the U.S. Navy. He is also very well trained in many fields of science.

Captain Venture had a significant change in his thinking when clear scientific evidence convinced him of creation. He now believes that a Master Designer put the universe into place. Before this time, the Captain, like many other scientists of his day, was told that only evolution could be scientific. As a creation scientist he now believes in the historical truth of Scripture. This has given Captain Venture a new outlook toward science and the interpretation of scientific data.

This book describes an exciting voyage of the space shuttle. Captain Venture and two specially selected student companions will be studying many fascinating things about astronomy and the stars. The adventure begins on planet Earth where Jonathan and Ann, Captain Venture's student companions, will begin learning some basic astronomy facts in preparation for their Voyage to the Stars.

Voyage to the Stars is designed to make interesting reading in science, present accurate information about the stars and astronomy, be used as supplementary reading in science, and above all, to glorify and acknowledge the magnitude and majesty of our Creator.

Chapter **1**

MEETING THE CAPTAIN

Photo courtesy of U.S. Air Force Academy Planetarium.

Jonathan and Ann, two young people chosen from a national science competition to be the first teenagers in space, walked up the pathway to the Air Force Planetarium at Colorado Springs, Colorado. Both were wondering what Captain Venture, the leader of their mission, would be like.

"I've seen pictures of him, but I've never seen him in person," said Ann.

"Same here," responded Jonathan. "I heard he was the youngest astronaut NASA ever had."

Their nervousness caused them to stop talking altogether as they neared the planetarium offices. After checking with the receptionist, they started for the door marked "Capt. A.D. Venture." Before they could knock, however, Captain Venture opened his door. The tall, young, uniformed Captain held out his hand to them and said, "Well, here are my student space companions. I was just on my way out to meet you! We're going to have a great time!"

Ann and Jonathan looked at each other and then back at the Captain. He was smiling and said, "I have planned some interesting experiences for us, but we have a lot of work to do before Discovery leaves the launch pad a few days from now. Everything I have heard about you tells me you're up to the job. We'll be working as a team in space, so I want you to

ask every question that comes to mind. Remember, there is no such thing as a dumb question. I won't have all the answers, but we can search for answers together. How does that sound to you?"

Jonathan said, "Sounds like you want us to be real scientists, Captain." Ann nodded in agreement.

"Science involves a 'search for truth,' so we have to keep an open mind at all times. The key to the scientific method is to use the skills of doing science correctly."

As they entered the new planetarium dome, Ann asked, "Captain, you worked with the new Hubble space telescope, isn't that right?"

"Yes, Ann, I have," he replied.

"Could you tell us something about it?"

Captain Venture's eyes lit up. "I can and I will!" he exclaimed. "Let's make this the first part of our getting acquainted session. Please have a seat and make yourself comfortable." Ann

> PROCESS SKILLS OF SCIENCE ARE THE SKILLS A SCIENTIST USES SUCH AS:
> · OBSERVATION
> · CLASSIFYING
> · MEASURING
> · EXPERIMENTING
> · INFERRING
> · PREDICTING
> · FORMING MODELS
> · INTERPRETING DATA

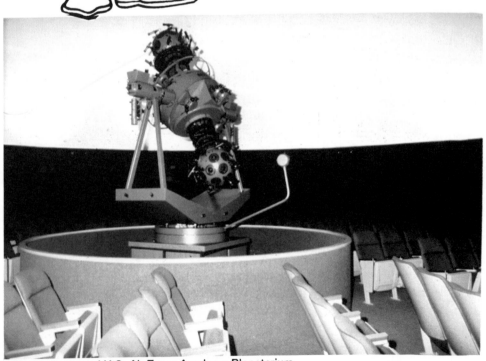

Photo courtesy of U.S. Air Force Academy Planetarium.

and Jonathan could tell this was one of Captain Venture's favorite projects. "Several very complex instruments were placed on board the telescope; these instruments were designed to analyze light in a special way. This outstanding telescope is a masterpiece of space technology. Let me explain a little about the structure of this telescope from this model." Holding a model of the telescope in front of him, he continued.

"The only unfortunate thing related to this telescope is its focusing. Once NASA placed the telescope into orbit they found that it did not focus clearly. The NASA scientists saw their mistake. They plan to correct this problem soon." The captain looked a little sad at this point, but went on to say, "In spite of this, one of the greatest things about the Hubble Telescope is that scientists won't have to worry about bad viewing because there won't be any of Earth's atmosphere to look through."

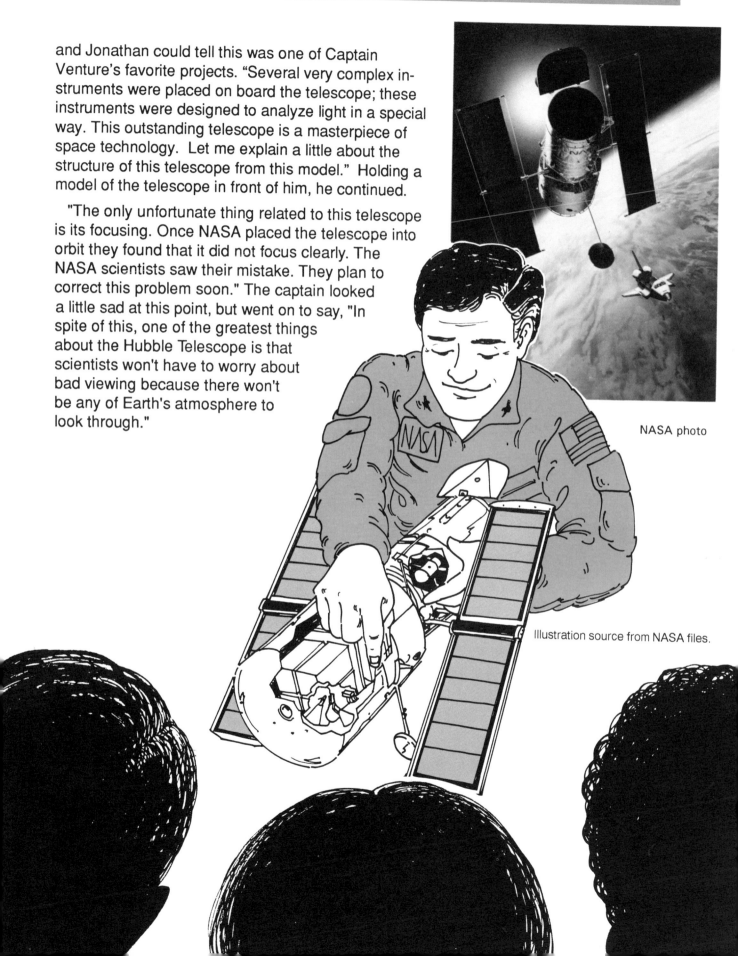

NASA photo

Illustration source from NASA files.

MAGNITUDE:
THE ASTRONOMERS' RULE FOR BRIGHTNESS.

THE POGSON SCALE:
ZERO MAGNITUDE WAS ASSIGNED TO A GROUP OF STANDARD STARS NEAR THE NORTH CELESTIAL POLE. THIS WAS KNOWN AS THE NORTH POLAR SEQUENCE. NOW PHOTOELECTRIC MEASUREMENTS ARE USED.

TRY YOUR MATH ON THIS SCALE IF YOU CAN.

After allowing Ann and Jonathan to examine the model space telescope, Captain Venture pointed to a magnitude chart. He said, "The new telescope will be able to see a star with a brightness of the 29th magnitude. I don't have to tell you that represents a very dim star. With our present telescopes, we can see stars up to about the 24th magnitude from the earth."

THE POGSON SCALE

Apparent Magnitude Difference In Star Brightness		
1st Magnitude	2.5	Times
2nd Magnitude	6.3	Times
3rd Magnitude	15.8	Times
4th Magnitude	39.8	Times
5th Magnitude	100.0	Times
* 6th Magnitude	**251.0**	Times
7th Magnitude	631.0	Times
8th Magnitude	1585.0	Times
9th Magnitude	3981.0	Times
10th Magnitude	10,000.0	Times
11th Magnitude	25,125.1	Times
(cont.)	??????.?	Times

Starting with 1st magnitude and the number 2.512, for every increase in magnitude by one factor, the brightness **decreases 2.512** times. What would be the brightness factor of a 15th magnitude star? Think of our own sun as having a magnitude of 4.8 and one of our very brightest stars, Sirius, the Dog Star, as having a brightness of −1.46.

*The naked eye can just see a 6th magnitude star.

(2.512 x 2.512 = 6.31 and 6.31 x 2.512 = 15.85)

Jonathan commented, "I guess the idea of magnitude isn't too clear to me."

"Think of it simply as a term that the astronomers use to indicate the brightness of a star, although the idea of magnitude can become very complex as astronomers seek to make the study of stars more precise," said Captain Venture.

"What about the term 'apparent magnitude'?" asked Jonathan.

"Jonathan, this term is very important to astronomers.

What we see from earth is **apparent magnitude**. If we actually knew the distance of the star from the earth, we could calculate its **absolute magnitude**.

"Look at the magnitude scale and see if you can work out the mathematics. With the new space telescope, we will not only see objects at greater distances, but stars will appear very sharp instead of fuzzy."

Jonathan noticed something in the picture that puzzled him. "Captain, I thought stars were just points of light. I was told that even the largest telescope couldn't magnify a star."

"That's right, Jonathan, even the Hubble cannot magnify a star."

Jonathan pointed to the picture and said, "Look at the size of that star, that's no point of light."

APPARENT MAGNITUDE IS HOW WE SEE A STAR'S BRIGHTNESS FROM EARTH.
ABSOLUTE MAGNITUDE IS RELATED TO THE STAR'S DISTANCE. WHENEVER YOU HEAR AN ASTRONOMER USE THE WORD LUMINOSITY, HE IS REFERING TO ABSOLUTE MAGNITUDE.

Part of the star cluster NGC 3532 as seen from Earth (left) and from Hubble. In spite of the Hubble Space Telescope focusing problem, you can see it produces much better pictures than from the ground.

Captain Venture laughed and said, "You are very good at observation, Jonathan. What you are looking at is a point of light that has been recorded electronically. The longer the film is exposed to the light from the star, the more of its light you will see. Now do you understand why some of the stars in the Hubble photo seem so big?"

"Yes," said Jonathan. "And now I understand that brighter stars will appear larger in a photograph."

"And the Hubble telescope is making the study of stars easier!" exclaimed Ann.

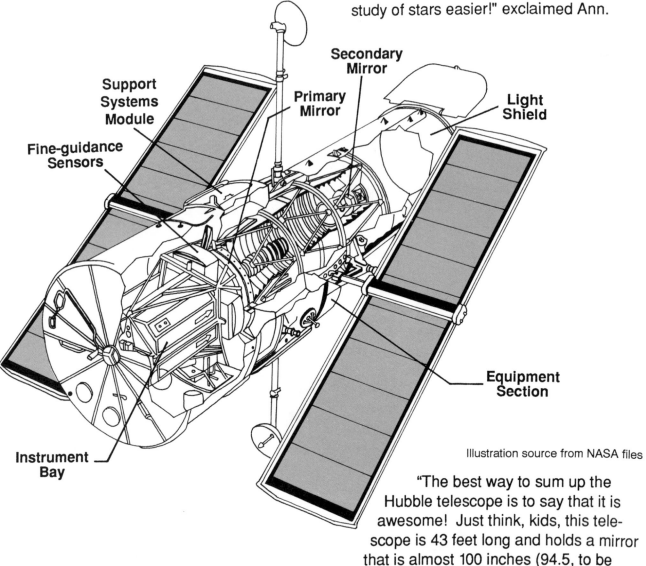

Illustration source from NASA files

"The best way to sum up the Hubble telescope is to say that it is awesome! Just think, kids, this telescope is 43 feet long and holds a mirror that is almost 100 inches (94.5, to be exact) in diameter. The Hubble is now in orbit 370 miles above the earth."

"That is about as far as the distance between Memphis and Chattanooga!" exclaimed Ann.

"Only straight up," added Jonathan.

Ann and Jonathan could see that Captain Venture had a special interest in this new $1,500,000,000 telescope. The fact that he had spent hundreds of hours on this project became apparent as he went on to describe all of the special parts that would be on board the telescope.

"Well, I could talk about this new instrument for a long time, but we have to get started with the preparations for our voyage, and we will not be using the Hubble for our particular mission."

Captain Venture paused a moment, then said, "Although we have been able to build some very impressive machinery, what really impresses me are the things that these instruments enable us to see."

Ann and Jonathan were thankful Captain Venture believed in the Creator, just as they did. He seemed to know so much. "It's been good to get acquainted," the Captain said. "Our first official briefing session will begin in the main dome of the Planetarium tomorrow morning at 0700."

THE MILITARY CLOCK

```
0100 HRS. = 1:00 A.M.
0700 HRS. = 7:00 A.M.
1200 HRS. = 12:00 NOON
1500 HRS. = 3:00 P.M.
2000 HRS. = 8:00 P.M.
2400 HRS. = 12:00 MIDNIGHT
```

1. WHAT ARE THE SKILLS THAT ARE USED BY SCIENTISTS?

2. WHAT DOES THE WORD "MAGNITUDE" MEAN WHEN WE OBSERVE STARS?

3. WHICH IS THE BRIGHTER, A FIRST MAGNITUDE STAR OR A 20th MAGNITUDE STAR?

Chapter **2**

THE BRIEFING ROOM

At precisely 0700, Captain Venture was ready for the first briefing session at the Planetarium. Jonathan and Ann were in their seats ready for some hard studying. They knew this would prepare them for their important voyage to the stars. Captain Venture made it clear that the purpose of the briefing would be to give Ann and Jonathan important background information in order to understand what they were about to see in outer space. He wanted their voyage to the stars to be very successful and very special. Most of all, he wanted them to see God's handiwork in space.

"Some of the information you will hear in this briefing," began Captain Venture, "you may have already studied in your science classes. It is not difficult to understand. The one thing I am sure will be new and exciting will be our trip into orbit with the space shuttle. We will also go through specialized training to prepare for the trip. First of all, I want you to meet the pilots." Captain Venture motioned to the two young men who had been sitting near the back of the room. "This is Major Stephen Paul, the command pilot of this spacecraft and his second-in-command, Captain Richard Brock."

Major Paul introduced himself. "We are anxious to welcome you aboard the Discovery spacecraft. It is on the launch pad going through final preflight check. Since this will be your first flight into space, we have several

things to talk about. One of these is **escape velocity**."

"What is **escape velocity**?" asked Ann.

"The speed of our space ship must always be slower than Earth's escape velocity. If we reached escape velocity, we would escape the Earth's gravitational attraction and never come back," said Major Paul.

Air Force Academy Planitarium

NASA Photo, Kennedy Space Center, Cape Canaveral, Florida

Captain Brock interrupted to explain this idea a little further. "Every object, whether large or small, must reach the same speed in order to escape the earth's gravity. Even gas molecules such as helium and other gases have to reach the escape velocity of a planet in order to get out of its gravitational field.

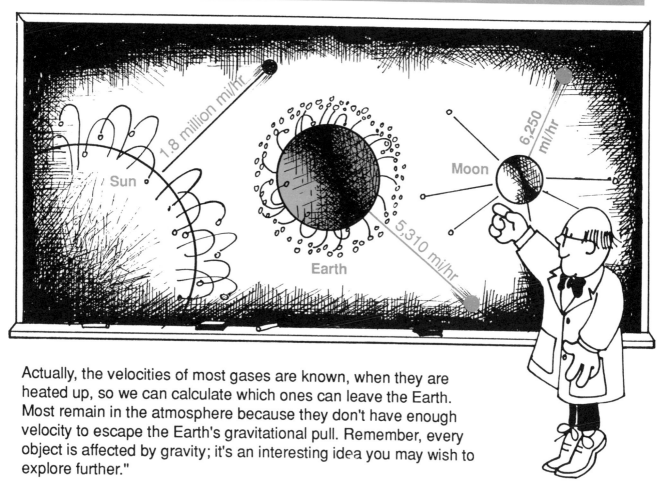

Actually, the velocities of most gases are known, when they are heated up, so we can calculate which ones can leave the Earth. Most remain in the atmosphere because they don't have enough velocity to escape the Earth's gravitational pull. Remember, every object is affected by gravity; it's an interesting idea you may wish to explore further."

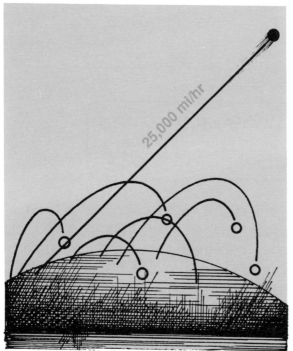

Gas particle escaping the earth's atmosphere after reaching its escape velocity. (25,000 mi/hr)

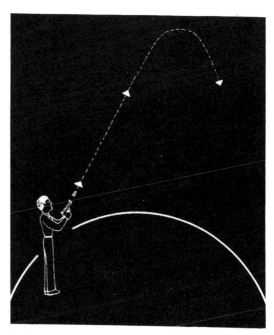

Bullet not arriving at escape velocity returns to earth.

Captain Brock continued, "The escape velocity for earth is approximately (11 km/sec) 25,000 mi/hr. We won't be going that fast because we don't want to leave the earth forever. Our speed will be approximately 17,500 miles per hour. This is our entry speed for a low orbit, and is the best speed for our mission. Speaking of speed, we can be glad that we aren't on the sun.

Sun

THE SPEED OF A GAS MOLECULE IS RELATED TO ITS TEMPERATURE AND ITS MASS. SOME GASES DON'T MOVE VERY FAST WHEN THEY ARE HEATED, OTHERS MOVE EXTREMELY FAST. THE FAST ONES CAN ESCAPE THE EARTH'S ATMOSPHERE.

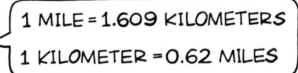

1 MILE = 1.609 KILOMETERS

1 KILOMETER = 0.62 MILES

"On the sun our escape velocity would have to be (617 km/sec) over 3 million mi/hr. This is over 53 times greater than our velocity of escape from earth." Ann and Jonathan looked surprised. Captain Brock explained. "Remember, you could fit a million earths into the sun, so this gives some idea of the size of the sun as it relates to the earth. Imagine how much greater the gravitational pull would be on the sun!"

1,000,000 Earths would fit into our sun's volume.

"Now that we've discussed escape velocity a little, let's talk about our orbit." The Major emphasized that it would be necessary to bring the space shuttle into a nearly perfect orbit. "If we do not obtain enough velocity, this would cause the shuttle to fall back to Earth too quickly. If we exceed the velocity needed, we will go into a hyperbolic path, which would sail us off to the stars. Well, actually, we would be captured by the Sun."

"Does this mean we would orbit the sun?" asked Ann.

"Yes, Ann, that's correct," said Major Paul. "As you can see, neither of these orbits would mean a successful mission." The Major could see that Jonathan and Ann looked worried, so he changed the subject.

Two objects of different size can have the same mass.

THE VAN ALLEN RADIATION BELTS ARE AREAS OF RADIATION THAT RANGE FROM 620-3,100 MI. IN THE LOWER BELT TO 9,300-15,500 MI. IN THE UPPER BELT. THESE VAN ALLEN BELTS LOOK SOMETHING LIKE THIS DRAWING. THEY ARE VERY HIGH ENERGY BELTS AND WOULD SEVERELY INJURE HUMAN FLESH.

YOU CAN'T SEE THROUGH AN OBJECT LIKE THE EARTH, CAN YOU?

"Actually," added Major Paul, "we will place the orbiter in position so that we can see as much of the sky as possible at one time. We can do this by reaching an altitude of about 500 miles. We have to be careful that we don't run into the Van Allen radiation belts, though."

"I remember reading about those areas of space. They're quite dangerous, aren't they?" Ann had a doubtful expression on her face.

"That's right, Ann. We wouldn't want to stay in them very long, and, actually, we don't plan to get into them at all!"

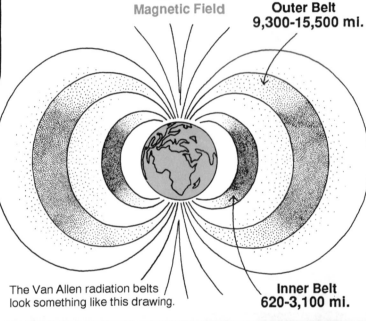

Earth's Magnetic Field

Outer Belt 9,300-15,500 mi.

Inner Belt 620-3,100 mi.

The Van Allen radiation belts look something like this drawing.

Earth Orbiter path showing blind spots.

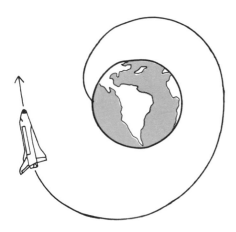

A hyperbolic path is achieved when escape velocity is reached. Orbiter would leave the Earth and be captured by the Sun.

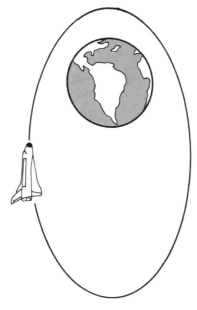

An elliptical orbit is reached with too little velocity for escape. This orbit is the standard orbit for the shuttle.

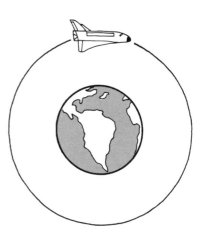

A circular orbit is reached with the correct velocity.

"We would probably get fried by the radiation if we did, wouldn't we?" asked Jonathan, watching to see how Ann reacted.

"Well," answered the Captain, "this is why we avoid getting into them; we don't want to find out."
Captain Venture continued, "In comparison to our planned orbit of 500+ miles, the Hubble space telescope will orbit around the earth at a distance of 370 miles. The Earth will get in the way of its vision much of the time. Our orbit will give us a little better vision. It will be worth the extra fuel we'll have to use to get there. As you probably guessed, we have modified our solid rocket boosters (SRB) and shuttle main engines (SME) for this purpose.

Major Paul added, "We will also be able to turn the orbiter in any position once we are in a fixed orbit around the earth. We have the best gyro compasses in the world on board. Who knows the difference between a gyrocompass and a regular magnetic compass?"

Jonathan answered, "I know the magnetic compass always points to the Earth's magnetic pole. I think the gyrocompass always points in the direction it is set; is that right, Captain?"

Both Jonathan and Ann were beginning to see that their space flight would require much homework.

Hubble Space Telescope.

Ann had some other questions to ask Major Paul. She burst out with one that was foremost on her mind. "What would happen if we were struck by a meteorite on our way into orbit?"

"Well," stated Major Paul, "we hope that won't happen. Even if it did, it is not likely it will knock us out of the sky.

"Actually," he went on, "we will no doubt collide with small space particles on our voyage. They won't be large enough to hurt us, but they may put a dent in our spaceship."

This made Ann feel a little better about the trip, but she still prayed that the Lord would protect them. She also had confidence that God would be in control, and remembered a Bible verse she had learned long ago: "If I ascend up into heaven, thou art there; . . ." (Psalm 139:8)

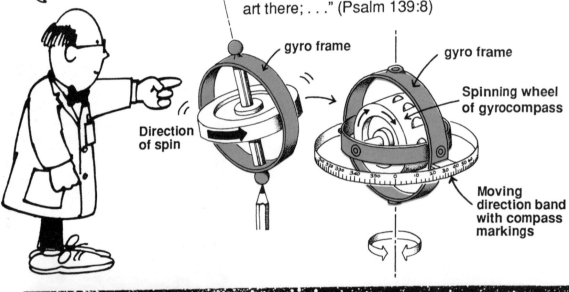

A GYROCOMPASS WORKS MUCH LIKE A REGULAR COMPASS IN THAT IT POINTS IN A CERTAIN DIRECTION; HOWEVER, THE GYRO COMPASS DEPENDS ON A WHEEL THAT IS SPINNING AT HIGH SPEED. AIRPLANES USE THE GYROCOMPASS FOR NAVIGATION.

gyro frame

Direction of spin

gyro frame

Spinning wheel of gyrocompass

Moving direction band with compass markings

This is an artist's drawing of space particles. In reality, even a fleck of paint at these speeds would put dents in the spacecraft. If they were as large as indicated in the drawing, they would seriously damage the shuttle.

Major Paul went on to explain that almost everything they did on the voyage was affected by their **relative position** and **motion**.

Jonathan wasn't quite sure he understood. "What do you mean by relative position and motion, sir?" he asked.

The earth is directly above the observer.

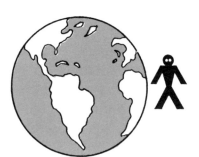

The earth is to the right of the observer.

The earth is beneath the observer.

The space shuttle is stationary to the observer.

The space shuttle is moving away from the observer.

Relative position and relative motion. Notice that the observer has a different viewpoint from different positions.

Captain Brock responded to Jonathan's question by saying, "Relative position really means where we are in relation to something else. You see, we must use reference points all along our journey to keep track of our position. We will be depending on the gyrocompasses in the spacecraft to point us to our target. When we get in space, we will have to depend upon other objects in the sky, such as stars and constellations, to get a fix on our position."

Jonathan said, "That's because the motion of the stars is so dependable, isn't it?"

"That's correct, Jonathan. Navigators have learned they can rely on the consistent, orderly movement of stars and planets," said Captain Brock.

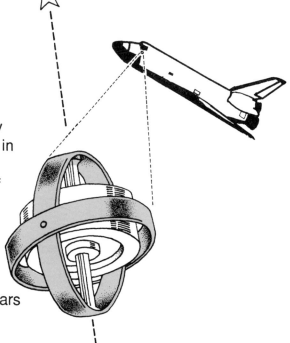

The gyrocompass keeps a fixed position for our spacecraft to navigate from.

"Well, I can't think of anything else that we need to bring up at this time. Captain Venture, I think it's time to turn the meeting back to you."

Major Paul and Captain Brock smiled, saluted Ann and Jonathan, and walked out of the room.

Captain Venture then turned to Ann and Jonathan and said, "It's a rare privilege for us to accompany these men on this scientific expedition. Remember, our objective is to make sure that the scientific data we bring back are accurate. Assumptions are not facts. Often scientists get carried away with their assumptions.

"Even seasoned scientists often want to believe something so badly that their assumptions are stated as though they are factual. Some scientists believe that evolution is a fact even though there are no scientific data to demand it.

"A true scientist doesn't make an assumption sound like a fact!"

STOP FOR QUESTIONS

1. WHAT IS A GYROCOMPASS?

2. WHY ARE THE VAN ALLEN RADIATION BELTS DANGEROUS?

3. WHY CAN'T WE SEE ALL OF THE SKY ALL OF THE TIME WHEN WE ARE IN ORBIT?

4. WHAT DOES RELATIVE POSITION MEAN IN OUR VOYAGE TO THE STARS?

WHEN YOU ARE IN SPACE, THERE IS NO PLANET SPINNING UNDER YOUR FEET.

Chapter **3**

GETTING UP TO DATE

Captain Venture said, "Ann and Jonathan, it's time for you to review your knowledge of important points in space. Let's start with a little review of astronomy. I've placed some books and other materials at your desks."

Captain Venture continued, "We will be using the **celestial sphere**, **Polaris**, the **celestial equator**, and some of the major **constellations** as reference points. Because this terminology will be very important, I want you to do some homework. We will be using these terms to locate special places in the heavens for our study. There is another thing we all have to understand. When we are on planet Earth, we can't see all the stars in the sky. Do you know how much we can see?" asked Captain Venture.

Jonathan responded quickly. "From horizon to horizon!"

"That's right, Jonathan, you learn very well. In fact," continued Captain Venture, "those stars that we can see from the northern hemisphere seem to be spinning around the North Star (Polaris). You will notice, however, when we get into space, orbiting planet Earth, we can see almost all the stars. None of these stars will rotate around the Pole star when we are viewing them from the orbiter. These drawings will help you to understand more about this idea.

"Things are going to be quite different for us on the orbiter than they are in these drawings. Also, in order to get ready for this mission, you will have to become very familiar with the terminology."

Jonathan said, "Don't worry about that, Captain Venture. Both Ann and I have had a lot of experience in our astronomy clubs. Everyone in my club studied in the school's new planetarium. Astronomy is so much fun that learning new terminology is easy."

"I'm glad to hear you say that," said Captain Venture. "This will make our briefing time much easier. By the way, there is one other relative position that we will be concerned with on Earth and also on the space platform. This position is the **zenith** and the **horizon line**. I will make some drawings to help you with this idea, too.

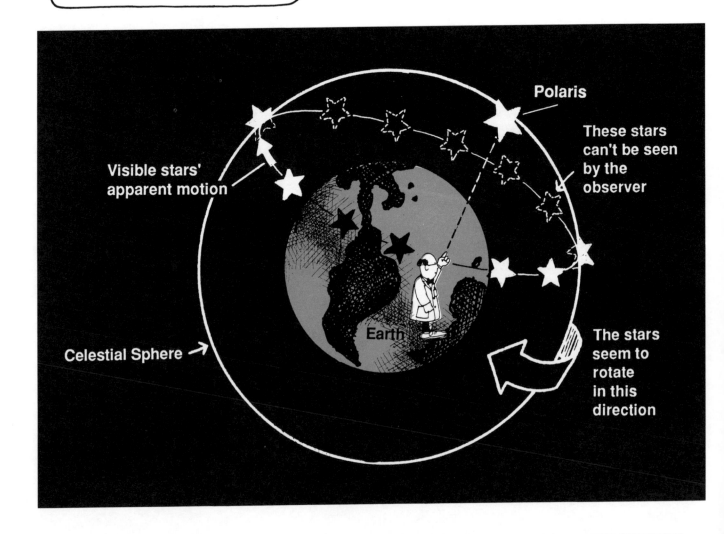

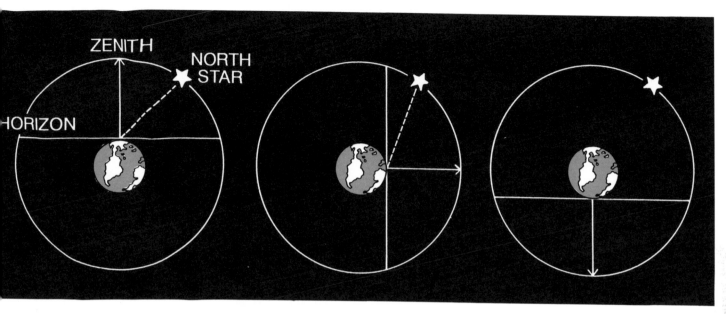

Notice that both zenith and horizon lines change with our position on Earth. This is also true for our space platform; our zenith and horizon lines will change in relation to our position in orbit.

"By the way, don't forget our little review of **relative position and motion**. You are suddenly going to be thrust into space and things aren't going to be the same. You will experience weightlessness and loss of direction."

Captain Venture reminded the young scientists that this could become confusing to them at times. "There is a variety of other reference points from which to obtain our **relative position** in space. Let's look at them again."

THE ZENITH POINT IS ALWAYS OVER YOUR HEAD. IN OTHER WORDS, THE POINT EXACTLY ABOVE YOU IS THE ZENITH.

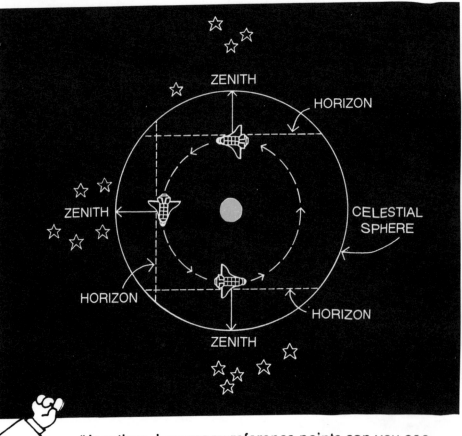

NOTICE THE HORIZON AND ZENITH CHANGES FOR THE ORBITER IN RELATION TO WHERE THE ORBITER IS AT THE MOMENT.

"Jonathan, how many reference points can you see in this drawing of the **celestial sphere**?"

Jonathan answered, "We can see the Earth's orbit around the Sun with the seasons. We can see that the **ecliptic** is in the same path that the sun takes across the sky each year. When we watch the sun's path during each day of the year, it is the same path that the Zodiac of the constellations takes at night. Twelve of the constellations, called the Zodiac, line up on the **ecliptic**.

Ann asked, "Captain Venture, did you notice that the **celestial equator** is tilted at 23 1/2° degrees from the ecliptic and the **Zodiac**?"

"Very observant, Ann. I can see why you won the science competition! Did you notice that the Zodiac is divided into twelve parts? These constellations in the band are part of the **signs of the Zodiac**."

Captain Venture added, "These are the signs that are used by astrologers when they come to predict future events. Astrologers practice what we call a *pseudoscience*, or false science."

Ann firmly announced: "I stay away from even reading about astrology."

"Me, too," agreed Jonathan. "I don't even want to put that stuff in my brain. You know the old saying: 'Garbage In- Garbage Out'!"

"You're right, Jonathan," said Captain Venture. "But more than that, the Scripture looks upon astrologers as practitioners of satanic arts and warns us to watch out for this 'doctrine of the devil'."

Captain Venture looked at his watch. "Hmmm!" he exclaimed. "It's 1150. Let's break and come back at 1300. Our topic for the afternoon's briefing sessions will center on star distances."

THE CELESTIAL SPHERE IS AN IMAGINARY SPHERE OF GREAT SIZE. THIS SPHERE PROVIDES A SURFACE FOR PLACING VARIOUS CELESTIAL POINTS.

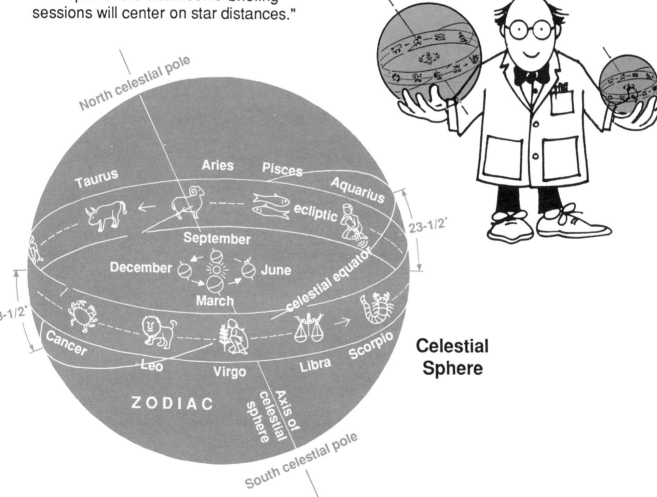

Celestial Sphere

The celestial sphere. The celestial equator is the extension of the earth's equator, and its poles are lined up with the north and south poles. The ecliptic is a great circle formed on the celestial sphere. It is inclined by 23-1/2 degrees to the celestial equator.

1. DRAW A ZENITH POINT FOR A MAN STANDING ON EARTH.

2. WHY CAN'T WE SEE THE SAME STARS IN THE SKY ALL YEAR 'ROUND?

3. WHY DO STARS SEEM TO SPIN AROUND THE NORTH POLE?

4. WHERE IS THE CELESTIAL SPHERE?

Chapter **4**

YARDSTICKS FOR SPACE

THE ASTRONOMICAL UNIT, PARALLAX, PARSECS, AND CEPHEID VARIABLES

It was exactly 1300 when Captain Venture walked back into the briefing room. Ann and Jonathan were already in their seats, talking about gyrocompasses.

Captain Venture began, "Our topic this afternoon will be how to tell distances in space. Let's start with the shortest unit of astronomical measurement, called the **Astronomical Unit** (AU). This is the distance between the Earth and the sun."

Jonathan said, "We learned in science class that the distance between the Earth and the sun is about 93,000,000 miles. Is that one Astronomical Unit?"

"That's correct, Jonathan. This unit is used when referring to distances between planets such as the Earth and the sun, 1 AU, and the sun and Jupiter, 4.9 – 5.4 AU.

Ann walked to the blackboard and began multiplying the average AU, 5.2 x 93,000,000. "That's 484 million miles!" she exclaimed.

Jonathan gave a long, low whistle. "That's a long, long way!"

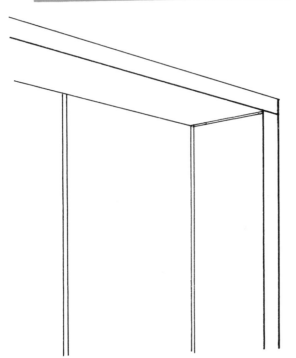

"It certainly is," responded the captain. "Believe it or not, this unit of measurement is too *small* to use with star distances; it is fine, however, for Earth-to-planet or planet-to-planet distances."

"Then, whenever we talk about planets, we should use the 'astronomical unit' for distances; is that right, Captain?"

"Correct, Ann." He smiled at his young scientist companions.

Both Ann and Jonathan were beginning to realize how interesting it was to talk with Captain Venture and to learn so much "scientific language." They had even decided to do a little research on their own.

"May we go to the library after the briefing session?" asked Jonathan.

"Sure can," said Captain Venture. "As a matter of fact, we have one of the finest libraries in the United States here at the U.S. Air Force Academy."

Captain Venture smiled and gave them directions. "See you in an hour," he said. One could see from Captain Venture's face he was enjoying the sessions as much as Ann and Jonathan.

Later that afternoon, Captain Venture started the last session with a little warning to the young astronauts. "What I have to discuss now will be difficult to understand. In astronomy, we will be using a different unit of measurement for stars."

Ann asked, "Is this because stars are so much farther away, Captain?"

"Yes, stars are so far away that even the distance between Earth and the nearest one cannot be easily measured with the Astronomical Unit."

Ann said, "If the Astronomical Unit is not adequate for measuring distances between stars, what type of measurement do we use?"

"Distances between stars are often measured in terms of light years," replied the Captain. "Now, I know we haven't said much about a light year, but simply, it's the distance that light travels in one year at a speed of 186,000 miles per second. Another measurement unit that is used for such great distances is called a **parsec**. This is the distance at which a nearby star shows an apparent change in angle of one arc second over a six-month period. A parsec is 3.3 light years.

1 AU

Astronomical unit = 93,000,000 miles

1 light year is the distance light travels at a speed of 186,000 miles per second.	60,000", or almost 1 mile

In one year, light travels 5,880,000,000,000 miles, or 63,240 AU. If one AU were equal to one inch (as in the block labeled AU above) one light year would equal 63,240 inches, or almost one mile. Remember, the light year deals with distance—not time.

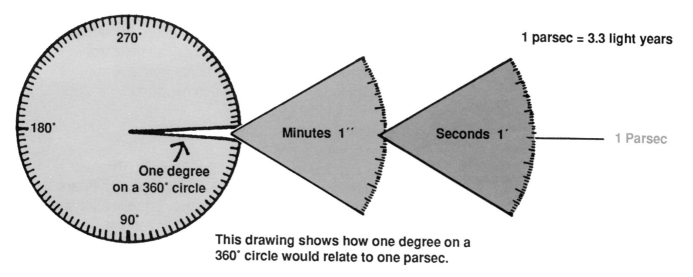

1 parsec = 3.3 light years

270°

180°

One degree on a 360° circle

90°

Minutes 1″

Seconds 1′

1 Parsec

This drawing shows how one degree on a 360° circle would relate to one parsec.

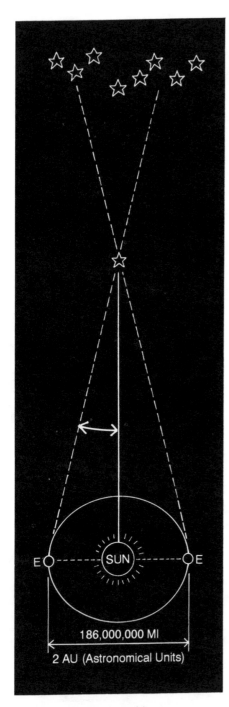

Using the Earth's orbit,
186 million miles, as a baseline,
present day astronomers can
achieve greater accuracy.

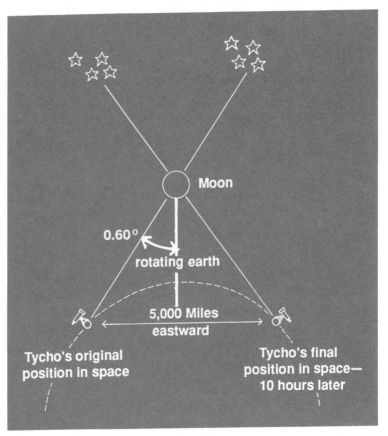

Tycho Brahe's first use of parallax. He used the moon as a reference point, and made his observations 5,000 miles apart.

"The system of calculating near distances is called **parallax**. Notice the drawings on our handout sheets. These will give you a clear picture of what we mean by parallax and parsecs," added the Captain.

"Actually, we can measure the distance to only about 700 stars by the parallax method because the others are too far away. Of course, this may change with the Hubble space telescope in operation. It will make observations much clearer, and may allow astronomers to make finer measurements than ever before. We will have to wait to see if this happens."

"How about the light year?"

"You told us that a light year is the distance light travels in one year," said Ann.

"I was coming to that," said the Captain. "The astronomical measurement that the average person hears most often is **'light year.'** This is the distance light can travel in one year at 186,000 miles per second. To be

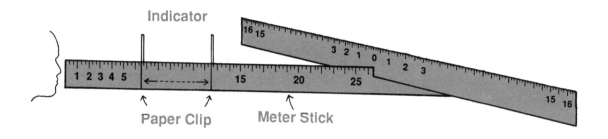

Indicator

Paper Clip   Meter Stick

Place your nose against the yard stick and look down the center of your indicator. Close one eye, and then the other. What happens? Move the indicator closer to the card. What happens? This is the way parallax is used, only on a much larger scale.

more precise, we say that it travels 299,792 kilometers per second. And, don't forget, the light year is a measurement of distance, not time."

It was Jonathan's turn to go to the blackboard this time. "I see what you mean, he said. "One light year is almost 6 trillion miles . And just think, some of the stars are 100,000 light years away!"

Captain Venture said, "Well, Jonathan, when objects are that far away, even the best scientists are doing a lot of guessing. There's one more method astronomers use for measuring distance. It's done with a star that appears to pulsate, called a **Cepheid**.

"The Cepheid variables are a large and very important

If you were observing a Cepheid variable star over a five-day period, you might see something like this (not to scale).

group of stars. These are very bright yellow giants or super giants that pulsate from very bright to dim within just a few days."

"How many of these are there?"

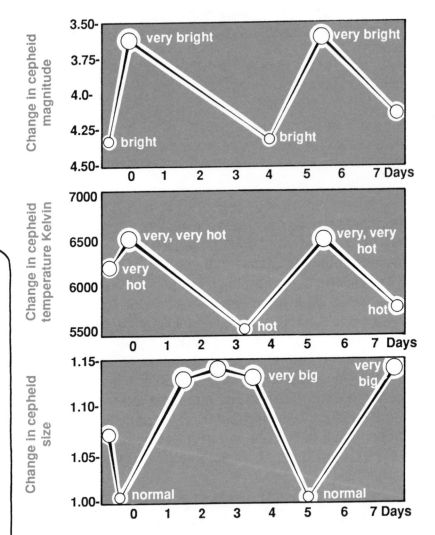

A typical Cepheid variable with a 7-day period would rise and fall something like this curve. Size, temperature, and brightness are shown here.

A CEPHEID VARIABLE IS A PULSATING STAR. NOW, ASSUMING THE PULSATIONS AND THE DISTANCES WORK HAND-IN-HAND, THEN THE ASTRONOMER CAN OBSERVE THE PULSATIONS AND CALCULATE WHAT THE DISTANCES MUST BE FOR STARS THAT ARE MUCH TOO FAR AWAY FOR THE PARALLAX METHOD. THE CEPHEID PULSATES BRIGHT AND DIM. BY WATCHING THE PULSES, ASTRONOMERS SAY THEY CAN DETERMINE THEIR BRIGHTNESS, AND FROM THEIR BRIGHTNESS THEIR DISTANCE.

"Good question, Ann. There are more than 700 in our galaxy, and many more outside our galaxy, of course. In fact, the distances of nearby galaxies from the earth are almost always calculated by Cepheid variable stars."

Jonathan interrupted, "Is this the most accurate system for measuring star distances?"

"No," said the Captain, "but it is useful to astronomers who believe in it. This is a case of one assumption leading to another."

Ann was trying her best to understand these great
star distances. She asked, "Captain Venture, if God
created the stars only thousands of years ago, how
can some of them be one hundred million light years
away? The light from a star at that distance wouldn't
have reached us yet."

"That is a good question, Ann," said Captain Venture. "Consider this. When God created the stars on
the fourth day (Genesis 1:14), He created the stars
and the light from them as a complete creation; this
included both the star and its light. We never see
anywhere in Scripture where God's creation is not
complete."

"I see," said Ann. The Captain
continued, "God had a purpose in
doing this. He tells us that He created them 'for signs and for seasons, and for days and years; and
let them be for lights in the heavens
to give light to the Earth'."

Jonathan added, "Of course, this
brings us back to our confidence in
the Word of God. If we believe the
Scriptures, then we must believe
what God said in them. If God were
there, then He would be the only
one who can tell us what really
happened."

"Come to think of it," said Ann, "it
also gives us a logical reason for

the universe as we see it."

"One other thing," said Captain Venture. "Can you imagine what a terrible time an evolutionist has explaining the mathematical order in the universe? Where did the order originate if an intelligent God did not create it? Of course, we ourselves do not have all the answers for all the questions, but that is why we try to encourage young scientists such as yourselves to continue exploring God's creation."

"We never dreamed we would be exploring in a spaceship!" beamed Jonathan.

At this point, Captain Venture dismissed the briefing with a parting comment, "0700 will come quickly. See you tomorrow."

STOP FOR QUESTIONS

1. WHAT IS AN ASTRONOMICAL UNIT?

2. WHAT DOES A LIGHT YEAR MEASURE?

3. GIVE AN EXAMPLE OF PARALLAX WITH YOUR OWN EYE.

4. HOW MANY LIGHT YEARS DOES A PARSEC REPRESENT?

5. HOW IS A CEPHEID STAR USED BY ASTRONOMERS?

Chapter 5
THE TELESCOPE: AN ASTRONOMER'S TOOL

NOTICE HOW THE LIGHT RAYS FROM THIS REFRACTOR ARE BENT TO A FOCUS POINT.

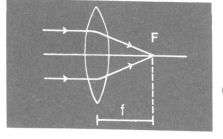

Convex lens

Both Jonathan and Ann were anxious for the next day's briefing. According to the schedule Captain Venture had given them, he would be talking about the composition of stars and how they could learn more about them at 0700.

Jonathan whispered to Ann, "He's never late."

"Shhh," Ann said. "We have a lot to learn."

Captain Venture began, "I am going to explain about the kind of equipment we will be using. Remember, an astronomer is only as good as his tools." He pointed to several pieces of astronomical equipment. "Our most important piece of equipment will be a mounted telescope. It is not as sophisticated as the Hubble, but I think you will be pleased and

Not until near the end of the last century was a telescope equipped with a 3-foot diameter lens. Today the world's largest refractor, shown above, is the 40-inch instrument at Yerkes Observatory in Williams Bay, Wisconsin.

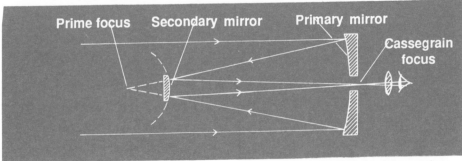

Light ray path in Cassegrain Configuration.

THE CASSEGRIAN TELE-
SCOPE IS THE MOST
POPULAR TELESCOPE
USED TODAY.

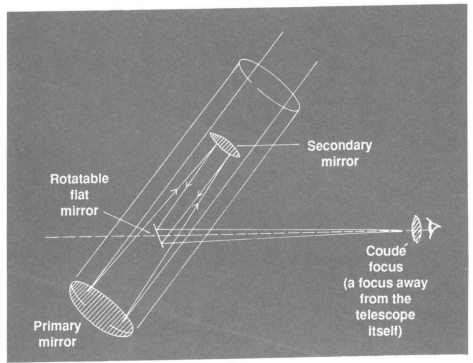

The light ray path in the Coudé configuration.

THIS IS A COUDÉ TEL-
ESCOPE WITH A MIRROR
THAT ROTATES WITH
THE MOVEMENT OF THE
OBJECT. NOTICE THAT
THE FOCUS POINT IS
AT A DISTANCE FROM
THE TELESCOPE.

surprised at what we will be able to see."

"What are these other telescopes for?" asked Jonathan.

"Even though we won't be using these, it will be good for you to get acquainted with them." Captain Venture handed out photographs of the telescopes. "Examine each one carefully," he said, "and you will have a better idea of what our special telescope will be doing," he said.

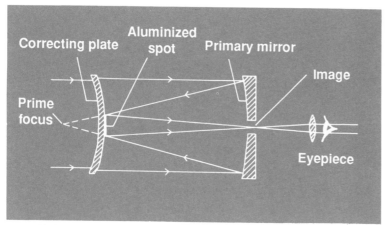

Light ray path in the Maksutov telescope.

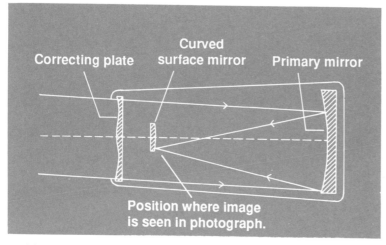

Light ray path in the Schmidt telescope. Actually, this telescope is a telescopic camera that takes in a wide field. The photographic plate is attached to the "curved surface mirror."

"By the way, Captain," interrupted Ann, "will you take a little time to explain what a **nova star** is?"

"A nova is a star that suddenly becomes very bright. It appears as though there is a sudden cataclysmic activity, like an explosion. This brightness intensifies, and then seems to die down to normal. Don't confuse this with a Cepheid variable star."

Captain Venture showed slides of a Cepheid variable in action. "The Cepheid variable is very predictable; the nova star is not. A nova would look something like

THIS IS A VERY COMPACT TELESCOPE. IT WAS INVENTED BY A RUSSIAN IN 1944.

THIS TELESCOPE WILL HELP PARTICULARLY IF THE ASTRONOMER WISHES TO SEARCH FOR COMETS AND NOVAS.

WHAT DIFFERENCE DO YOU NOTICE BETWEEN THE MAKSUTOV TELESCOPE AND THE SCHMIDT?

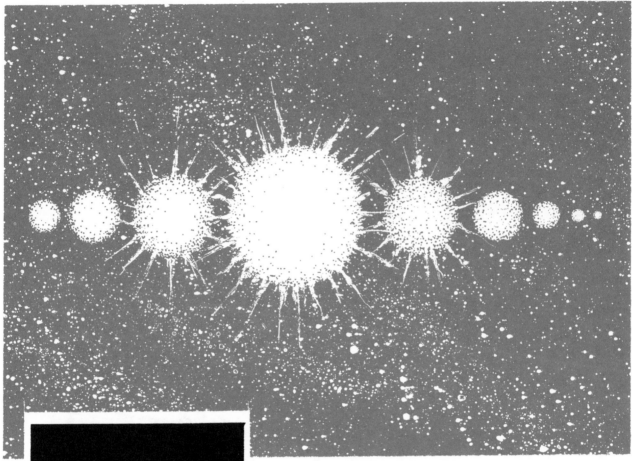

Artist's drawing of probable brighter stages of a nova star.

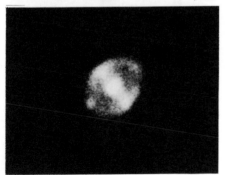

Nova Hercules – brighter stage

Nova Hercules—dim stage

this." The Captain showed them a drawing of Nova Cygni in 1975.

"It isn't likely that we will see a nova star act up while we are on this mission, but if it does, we certainly won't complain."

"That would be great!" said Jonathan.

"Well, I'm going to be looking for a nova star on our trip," said Ann decidedly.

Nova Hercules as it appeared in 1951.
(Hale Observatory)

This is an example of a nova star
in its erupting stage.

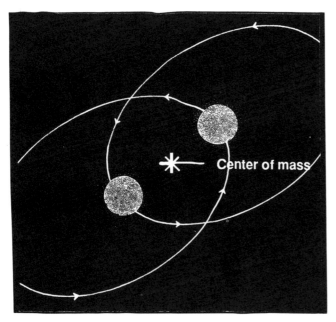

Fig A. Binary stars rotating around a center of mass. This diagram shows how two binary stars of the same mass might orbit each other. Sometimes they keep their distance; other times they swing close to each other, and then far away. In some cases, they actually touch and orbit around each other. They always obey the very precise laws of physics, such as gravitational attraction of two bodies toward each other.

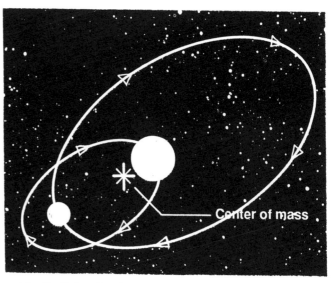

Fig. B. Notice that the center of mass shifts toward the larger of the two stars when the stars have significantly different masses.

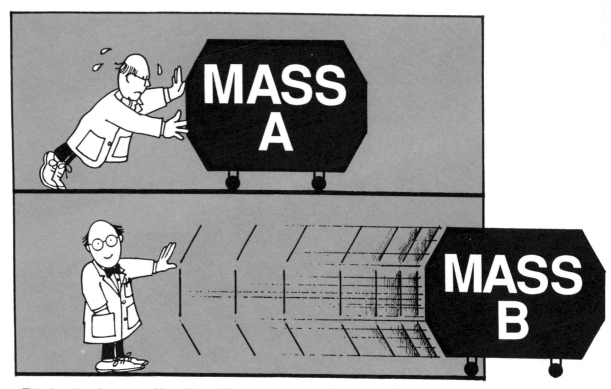

This drawing gives some idea of how different masses are affected by different amounts of effort (Mass A is greater than Mass B). This same idea applies to the masses of star systems. If they are the same, then the gravitational influence will be the same. If they are different, then the gravitational influence will be different.

What does the observer see when the dim star gets in front of the bright binary star?

What does the observer see when the bright star gets in front of the dim star?

STOP FOR QUESTIONS

1. WHY DO WE NEED DIFFERENT KINDS OF TELESCOPES?

2. WHAT IS THE DIFFERENCE BETWEEN A REFLECTING TELESCOPE AND A REFRACTING TELESCOPE?

3. WHAT DOES A NOVA STAR DO OCCASIONALLY?

4. CHOOSE THE TELESCOPE THAT YOU LIKE THE BEST. WHY DID YOU CHOOSE THIS ONE?

Chapter **6**
THE PARTING OF LIGHT

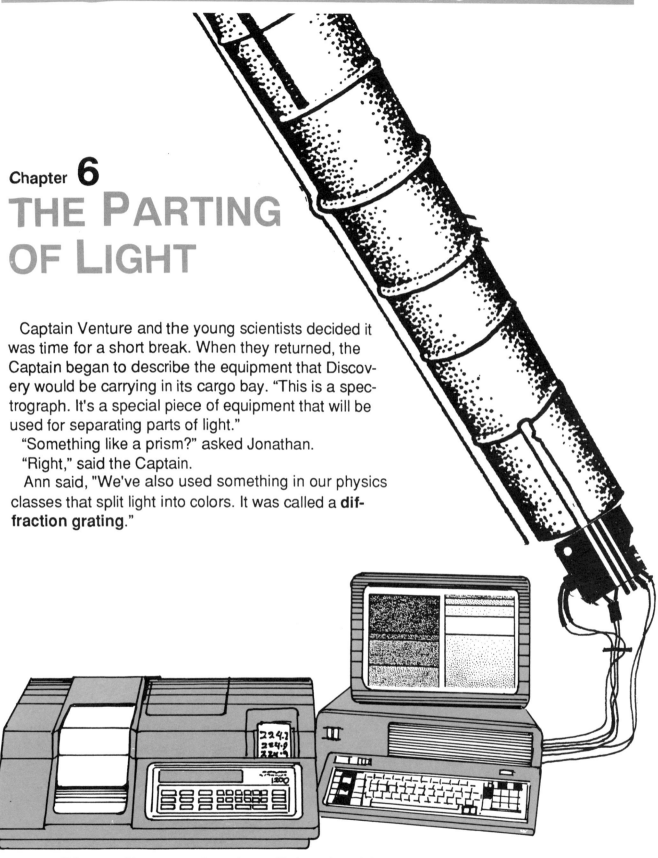

Captain Venture and the young scientists decided it was time for a short break. When they returned, the Captain began to describe the equipment that Discovery would be carrying in its cargo bay. "This is a spectrograph. It's a special piece of equipment that will be used for separating parts of light."

"Something like a prism?" asked Jonathan.

"Right," said the Captain.

Ann said, "We've also used something in our physics classes that split light into colors. It was called a **diffraction grating**."

Telescope with spectrograph attachment. Modern science laboratories use the spectrograph for analyzing unknown chemicals here on Earth. They can compare these observations with light coming in through the telescopes and make statements about a star's composition.

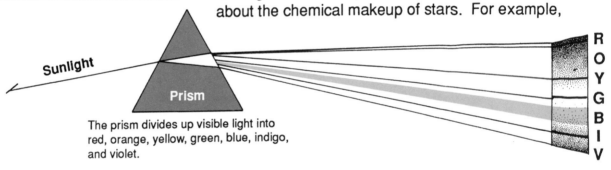

HERE'S A MNEMONIC TO HELP YOU REMEMBER: ROY G. BIV. RED, ORANGE, YELLOW, GREEN, BLUE, INDIGO, AND VIOLET.

"The spectrograph is more like the diffraction grating you referred to, and is a very important tool for the astronomer. He uses this instrument to study stars and other objects in the sky. Our telescope has been modified so we can attach a spectrograph."

Captain Venture continued, "Ann and Jonathan, this next part is difficult to understand. It is the subject of **spectroanalysis**. Let me explain a little about what we can find out from analyzing the spectrum. We know the spectrum is made up of many colors of visible light."

Ann asked, "Is this what God was referring to when He asked Job, 'By what way is the light parted?' " (Job 38:24)

"Yes it is, Ann. God knew what He had created, and He reminded Job of this."

Captain Venture went on to explain, "Actually, by looking at the color spectrum lines, we can tell much about the chemical makeup of stars. For example,

Sunlight

Prism

R O Y G B I V

The prism divides up visible light into red, orange, yellow, green, blue, indigo, and violet.

R O Y G B I V

glowing objects like the sun give out light in all different colors of the spectrum. Two German physicists discovered this was true through laboratory experiments. They discovered that the color of a heated object gave an indication of the temperature of that object. They concluded that if this were true in the science laboratory, then this same rule must also apply to other objects that glow — even stars.

"Astronomers now use this method to classify stars."

Captain Venture added, "When scientists look at

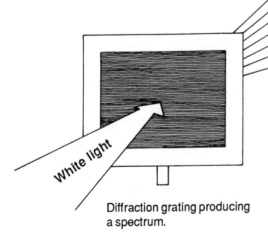

White light

Diffraction grating producing a spectrum.

the stars and other objects, the color differences become a source of important information. Our sun, for example, is in the yellow-green part of the spectrum, cooler stars look more reddish, and those that are hotter than the sun give off a blue light. We now use the color of the star, along with the spectrograph, to give us information about a star's chemical makeup. This information has helped us begin to understand why some stars shine so much brighter than others in the heavens."

Ann looked perplexed. "I can understand the spectrum and all of that, but how can this tell us about the star's chemistry?"

Captain Venture said. "Let me try to

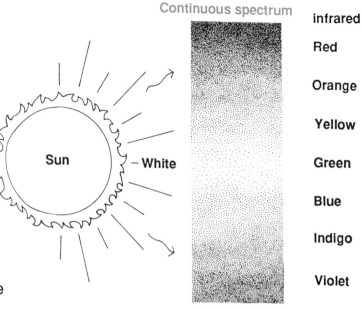

Continuous spectrum

infrared
Red
Orange
Yellow
Green
Blue
Indigo
Violet
Ultraviolet

Sun — White

Dark-line spectrum

Sun   Gas

Sunlight contains light of all colors, as does the light of any star.

OFTEN YOU WILL HEAR SCIENTISTS REFER TO THESE LINES AS FRAUNHOFER LINES. FRAUNHOFER DISCOVERED THESE VERY IMPORTANT LINES IN THE SPECTRUM. WE WILL BE REFERRING TO THESE LINES OFTEN WHEN WE ANALYZE THE STARS.

When sunlight from the sun's hot surface passes through cooler gases in the sun's atmosphere, certain light waves are absorbed, and dark lines appear.

explain how we discover which chemical element and compounds are contained in a system by using a spectrograph. When the sun's light passes through

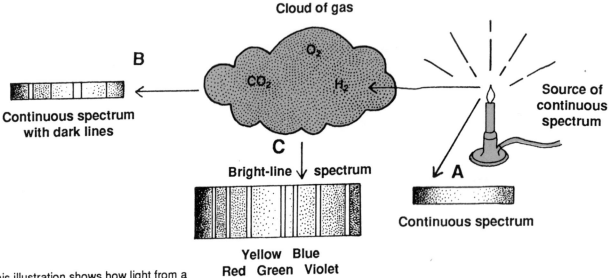

Cloud of gas

O_2

B

CO_2 H_2

Continuous spectrum with dark lines

Source of continuous spectrum

C

Bright-line spectrum

A

Continuous spectrum

Yellow   Blue
Red   Green   Violet

This illustration shows how light from a candle (star or planet) can be absorbed to form dark lines (B) from cool gases; the spectrum in (C) shows the bright lines produced from hot gases.

cooler gases such as carbon dioxide (CO_2), oxygen (O_2), hydrogen (H_2), and others, some of its light is blocked out and dark lines appear where a particular color in the spectrum would be."

"Oh!" exclaimed Ann. "An astronomer can tell what these elements are if he observes the location of the dark lines."

"Now you've got it!" exclaimed the Captain.

Ann said, "When I look at the spectrum, I am

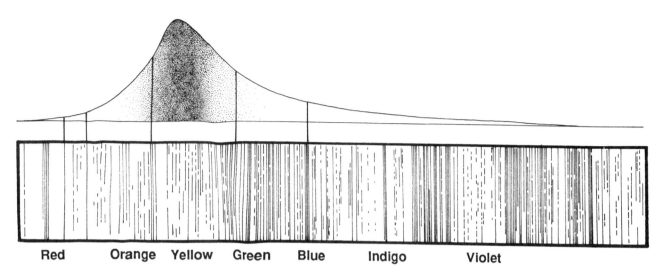

Red   Orange Yellow Green Blue   Indigo   Violet

Dark line spectrum

WHEN THE ASTRON-
OMER PHOTOGRAPHS
THE DARK LINE SPEC-
TRUM FROM THE SUN
AND THE BRIGHT LINE
SPECTRUM FROM THE
VARIOUS ELEMENTS,
HE CAN GET A GOOD
IDEA OF WHAT ELE-
MENTS ARE PRES-
ENT ON THE SUN.

amazed. This universe was created with purpose and order. The universe appears as though it were made from a blueprint. Scientists can examine the universe with confidence.

"Is this the same as when we analyze unknown elements in the chemistry and physics laboratories?"

"Yes, Ann, the difference is that we can't hold the object we are analyzing in our hands. We are talking about **absorption spectra**. This means just what it says. Some of the light of the spectrum is absorbed and dark lines appear in its place."

Ann said, "Then when we see these dark lines

appear, we usually know what's causing them. That's great!" They all nodded their heads in agreement.

Jonathan added, "It's great that we can depend on a God of order and purpose, one who holds the universe together. I don't see how evolutionists can ignore all the evidence."

Captain Venture looked at Jonathan and Ann for a moment. "The Apostle Paul gave some insight on this when he told the church at Rome: 'When they knew God, they glorified Him not as God, neither were thankful; but became vain in their imaginations, and their foolish heart was darkened.' I guess the best way to describe an evolutionist is to say that he is in darkness.

"Well, I'd rather talk about light than darkness! Tomorrow's topic will be the character of the sun, our nearest star. See you at . . ."

"Zero-seven-hundred!" And the two were gone out the door.

STOP FOR QUESTIONS

1. WHAT WORD IS USED FOR ANALYZING THE SPECTRUM?

2. OF WHAT IS THE VISIBLE SPECTRUM COMPOSED?

3. IN WHAT PART OF THE SPECTRUM IS OUR SUN'S LIGHT?

4. WHAT IS A FRAUNHOFER LINE?

Chapter 7

THE SUN: OUR NEAREST STAR

Zero-seven-hundred seemed to come very early the next morning for the young people. However, their tiredness was soon forgotten when Captain Venture began.

"Let's start the morning session with any questions you may have about the sun."

Ann asked, "What is the temperature of the sun, and what would happen if the sun were closer to the earth than it is now?"

"One question at a time, Ann. We are all aware of the great heat generated by our sun. Scientists have found that the surface temperature of the sun is about 6000 Kelvin (11,300° F). I am sure that you realize that such a temperature would vaporize most of the materials in our world. And this is only a fraction of the temperature *inside* the sun!"

Captain Venture continued, "If the sun is our **model** for the rest of the stars, then we can make predictions from this model. We can predict that the stars would be very hot gaseous bodies, also."

REMEMBER: WATER BOILS AT 212 DEGREES FAHRENHEIT.

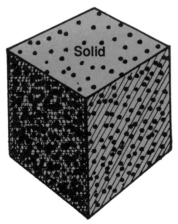

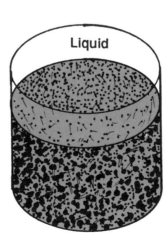

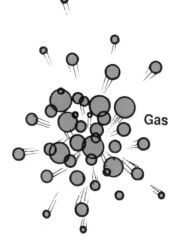

Three states of matter

A PREDICTION IS USUALLY MADE FROM FACTUAL DATA.

A MODEL IS A MANUFACTURED IMAGE OF SOMETHING – NOT THE REAL THING. MODELS CHANGE WITH NEW INFORMATION.

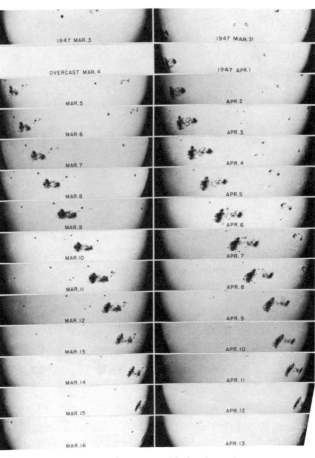

Sun spots showing the cooler areas. Notice how the spots seem to travel across the sun's sphere. (Palomar Observatory photograph)

Jonathan said, "I've also read in my science book that scientists predict there are storms of hot gas swirling and boiling on the surface of stars."

"That's absolutely correct, Jonathan. Here are pictures of our sun which show this. Furthermore, solar experts have measured sun spots, which are at cooler temperatures, ranging from 500 to 50,000 miles across."

"What do you mean by cooler temperatures, Captain?" asked Jonathan.

"By cooler, I mean the sun spots are about 8300° F. They appear as dark spots in these photographs."

Ann commented, "That's still very, very hot."

Captain Venture continued, "Sun spots increase and decline in an eleven-year cycle. In other words, sun spots reach a maximum number every eleven years.

"We also see storms that throw out hot gases. Some of these gases are thrown over 100,000 miles above the surface of the sun. Fortunately, the sun's gravity pulls most of them back to the sun's surface."

Solar flare

Closeups of sun spots. (Palomar Observatory photograph)

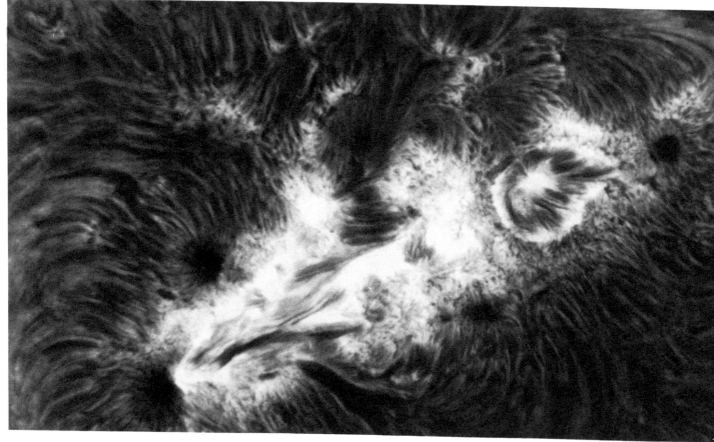

SUN

ONE ASTRONOMICAL UNIT (AU)
93,000,000 MILES

EARTH

Solar flares=high energy radiation, electrons-protons, neutrinos, infra red, ultra violet, cosmic rays, and radio waves.

Ann said, "I wonder what would happen if these gases escaped from the sun and struck the Earth?"

Captain Venture pointed out that in one sense they really do strike our planet. "When these violent solar flares occur," he explained, "our communications here on Earth are disrupted."

Jonathan looked thoughtful and said, "I can see why this evidence is important. Evidence like this would tell us that some of the radiation from the sun is escaping. This radiation would then strike the Earth's atmosphere and cause much damage to living things.

"I am glad that the sun isn't any closer to us, and our Creator knew exactly how far to place the sun from the Earth."

IF THE DISTANCE BE-TWEEN THE SUN AND THE EARTH WERE CLOSER, WE WOULD HAVE KILLING RADI-ATION, BURNING HEAT AND MAGNETIC STORMS.

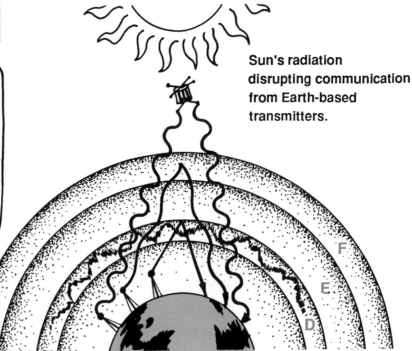

Sun's radiation disrupting communication from Earth-based transmitters.

During high sun spot activity, solar wind particles and high energy radiation break the ionosphere layers apart. When this happens, radio waves are blocked out. The "D" region is affected most. In more severe situations, the "E" and "F" regions are blocked out, also.

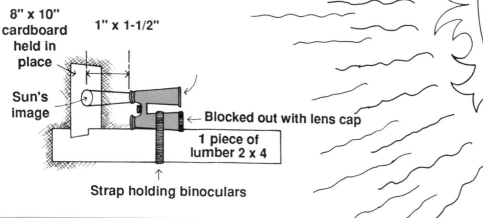

8" x 10" cardboard held in place

1" x 1-1/2"

Sun's image

Sun

← Blocked out with lens cap

1 piece of lumber 2 x 4

Strap holding binoculars

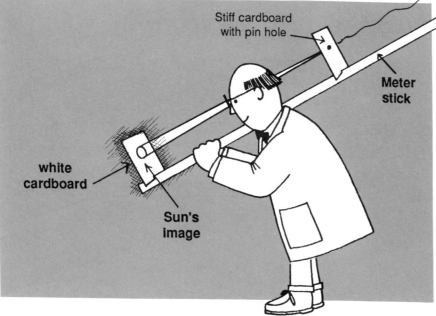

Stiff cardboard with pin hole

Meter stick

white cardboard

Sun's image

THERE ARE SAFE WAYS TO LOOK AT THE SUN. SOME OF THE IDEAS ABOVE WILL WORK FINE. DO NOT LOOK DIRECTLY AT THE SUN WITHOUT PROTECTION!

Captain Venture said, "We know a great deal about our sun, but we are a long way from having answers to all of the questions that we might ask. As we explore further, we are certain to come up with more answers. However, the sun can give us at least some idea of what the stars in our universe are like."

Ann asked, "Are you saying that we may have some surprises in store for us when we leave the Earth's atmosphere?"

Captain Venture replied, "Any scientific exploration is subject to unexpected surprises. Sometimes the unexpected opens up the way to new discovery. We will wait and see."

STOP FOR QUESTIONS

1. HOW FAR IS THE SUN FROM THE EARTH?

2. HOW DO SCIENTISTS USE MODELS?

3. IS A SUN SPOT THE HOTTEST PLACE ON THE SUN?

4. HOW OFTEN DO LARGE NUMBERS OF SUN SPOTS OCCUR?

Chapter **8**

FINDING
OUR WAY

When Ann and Jonathan returned to the Planetarium at 1300, Captain Venture was adjusting the overhead projector. He said, "This new topic will be a challenge to all of us. In order to find our way in the astronomical universe, we are going to need reference points. Ann, what are some of the reference points that we use from our position on Earth?"

Ann hesitated.

"Well," said the Captain, "what did we talk about earlier?" He was trying to make Ann and Jonathan apply what they had been learning.

Ann said, "What about the **north celestial pole**, **zenith**, and **ecliptic**? Can these be our reference guidelines?"

"Any more you want to add, Jonathan?"

"Sure," said Jonathan, "what about the constellations?"

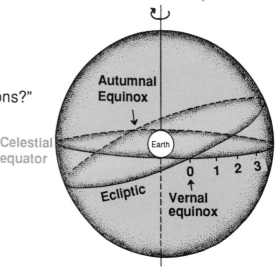

The vernal equinox is the time that the sun crosses the equator, March 23, in the spring (Vernal). The autumnal equinox is the time that the sun crosses the equator, September 22. Day and night are equal at these points.

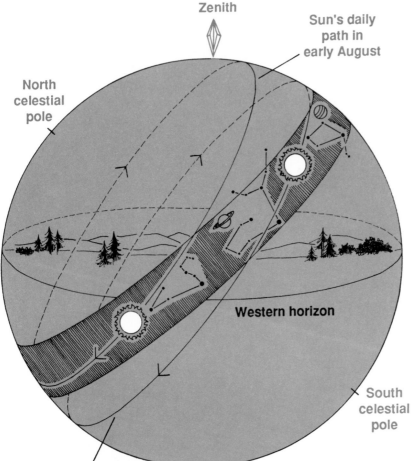

Zenith

Sun's daily path in early August

North celestial pole

Orbits of the sun, moon, and planets during the seasons give us a reference to the ecliptic.

Western horizon

South celestial pole

Sun's daily path in early October

"You have both listened well!" beamed Captain Venture as he switched on the planetarium projector and darkened the room. "This is the **ecliptic**, perhaps the most important point for us to remember."

Ann and Jonathan were amazed to actually see the line of the ecliptic on the Planetarium ceiling.

Then Captain Venture made the **celestial equator** line appear, as well as the **celestial poles**. Ann said, "It looks just like a sky with a road map on it!"

"Let's call the celestial equator, the extension of the earth's equator, the center of your sky road map. I would like you to look also at some other imaginary lines in the sky. This next projection will make the whole sky a latitude and longitude grid using the celestial equator.

Captain Venture threw a switch and the whole planetarium sky became a grid. He continued, "By using **spherical coordinates** on a sphere, we can find any spot in the sky just as we do on Earth. Notice that if you imagine the celestial equator as we do the equator here on Earth, we can find any point we want."

Ann said, "An easy way to find the ecliptic is to find the sun's path across the sky during one year. I remember that."

Jonathan interrupted, "I noticed the sun's position changes throughout the year."

"READ RIGHT UP." THAT'S A GOOD RULE FOR SPHERICAL COORDINATES. THIS IS ALMOST THE SAME FOR THE CELESTIAL SPHERE. FIRST READ RIGHT AND THEN READ UP.

FROM THIS POINT, WE CAN USE TERMS LIKE RIGHT ASCENSION AND DECLINATION, JUST AS WE USE LATITUDE AND LONGITUDE ON THE EARTH. NOW WE CAN LOCATE ANYTHING WE WANT IN THE SKY. JUST GIVE US THE RA (RIGHT ASCENSION) AND DEC. (DECLINATION).

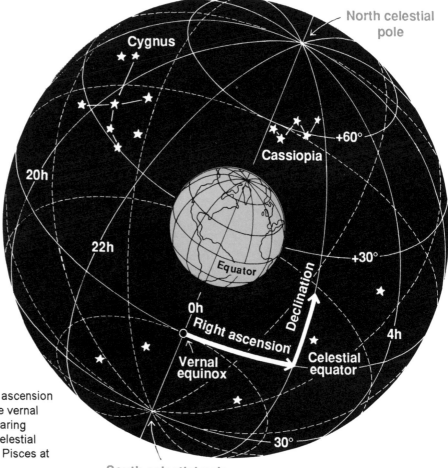

This celestial sphere shows how the right ascension and declination system is used. Notice the vernal equinox point; this is where the sun, appearing to move south to north, would cross the celestial equator. This is found in the constellation Pisces at the present.

ROMANS 1:20: FOR SINCE THE CREATION OF THE WORLD HIS INVISIBLE ATTRIBUTES, HIS ETERNAL POWER AND DIVINE NATURE, HAVE BEEN CLEARLY SEEN, BEING UNDERSTOOD THROUGH WHAT HAS BEEN MADE, SO THAT THEY ARE WITHOUT EXCUSE.

Jonathan said, "If that's true, then we should be able to follow the moon and planets at night to find the **ecliptic**."

"Good thinking, Jonathan! All of the other planets will fall on or near the **ecliptic**, except in the case of the planet Pluto."

Ann said, "If we can pinpoint locations in the sky by the **relative position** and **motion** of the sun and moon, that shows how orderly the universe really is."

"You're right, Ann," said Captain Venture. "It's impossible that this exactness and the laws that govern it happened by accident. You would think that even the most skeptical evolutionist would be forced to wonder where the order comes from."

Jonathan stared at the ceiling of the Planetarium where he could see the precise path of the planets. "I'm beginning to realize that God's power must be greater than we can imagine."

STOP FOR QUESTIONS

1. WHAT DOES THE PHRASE "READ RIGHT UP" MEAN FOR FINDING YOUR WAY?

2. COMPARE "LATITUDE AND LONGITUDE" WITH THE CELESTIAL COORDINATE TERMS "RIGHT ASCENSION AND DECLINATION."

3. WHERE IS THE ECLIPTIC IN THE HEAVENS?

4. WHAT PATH DOES THE ECLIPTIC FOLLOW?

Chapter **9**

THE SKYWAY TO OUR OBJECTIVE

Captain Venture stated, "The next part of our briefing session will deal with actual navigation. By using our reference point from Planet Earth we will sight the area of the sky we are interested in. In our case we are going to use some of the constellations as our objectives in the sky."

Captain Venture commented, "It is interesting that the book of Job, written over 4000 years ago, describes the constellations and stars so perfectly."

WHERE WERE YOU WHEN I LAID THE FOUNDATIONS OF THE EARTH?...
CAN YOU HOLD BACK THE STARS? CAN YOU RESTRAIN ORION OR PLEIADES? CAN YOU ENSURE THE PROPER SEQUENCE OF THE SEASONS, OR GUIDE THE CONSTELLATION OF THE BEAR WITH HER SATELLITES ACROSS THE HEAVENS? DO YOU KNOW THE LAWS OF THE UNIVERSE AND HOW THE HEAVENS INFLUENCE THE EARTH?

JOB 38:4; 31-33

The Pleiades are an open cluster of stars in the Constellation Taurus, The Bull.

Ann interrupted, "Here we are in modern times talking about the same constellations!"

"That's right," said the Captain. He went on to say, "The Pleiades, Orion, and the Great Bear are also mentioned in Scripture. Most of our viewing time, however, will be spent around the constellation Orion."

"What about the Great Bear?" asked Jonathan.

"The Great Bear, or Ursa Major, constellation is where the stars of the Big Dipper are found. The Big Dipper, also called Ursa Major, is used by navigators to locate the **north celestial pole**. Why would this be such an important point, Jonathan?"

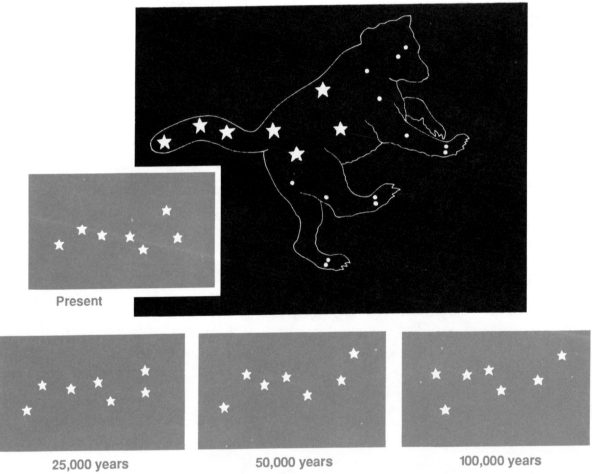

Present

25,000 years   50,000 years   100,000 years

Everything we presently know about the constellations seems to indicate that they are young. Today they are the very shapes that the ancient astronomers saw 4,000 years ago. This is true even though the stars in the "Big Dipper" (the Big Bear, Job 38:32) are moving away from each other at tremendous speeds. If the universe were billions of years old, then the stars in the "Big Dipper" would have looked differently in the past.

"That's easy, Captain Venture. The Earth is spinning and the **north celestial pole** acts just like the axle of a top." Captain Venture said, "Scientists have actually taken pictures of the night sky with their cameras pointed directly at the North Star, with the camera lens open for several hours. The constellations rotate in the night sky around this central point. The same is true for the **south celestial pole**. This gives you an idea about the reference points

NORTH CELESTIAL POLE
ZENITH
N
W
EARTH
E
CELESTIAL EQUATOR
S
OBSERVER'S HORIZON

NO MATTER WHERE THE BIG DIPPER IS AT ANY GIVEN MOMENT IN THE SKY, ITS POINTER STARS WILL ALWAYS POINT NEAR POLARIS (NORTH STAR).

POLARIS

The Big and Little Dipper turning around the North Star. Notice that the rest of the stars seem to rotate around Polaris.

USING THE **NORTH CE-LESTIAL POLE** AS A CENTER POINT OF REFERENCE, (FOUND IN THE HANDLE OF THE LITTLE DIPPER) GO DIRECTLY SOUTH, THROUGH THE MILKY WAY (OUR OWN GALAXY) AND BELOW THE **ECLIPTIC** TO FIND THE **CONSTELLATION** ORION.

God has placed in the sky that we use for navigational purposes. I am sure you will remember our studies in **relative position** and **motion**, and the need for a reference point.

"Well, we only have a few more things to cover in our briefings. Our main target is **Orion**, the Great Hunter. Once we locate this constellation, we should have no trouble finding other important galaxies and nebulae to study. Set your **Star Locator** and **Star Maps** on the Winter sky, and familiarize yourself as much as possible with the areas we will explore."

A star locator is an instrument used to locate stars and constellations at different times of the year.

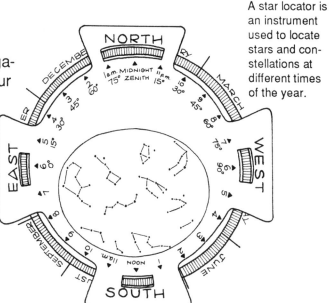

Jonathan said, "Someone told me one time that the story of the Gospel can be seen in the constellations. Is that right?"

"I've heard that too," said Ann. "It's like a sermon in the sky!"

"Glad you mentioned that," said the Captain. "Astrologers have corrupted the meaning of the constellations. But I believe, as do many others, that God placed the constellations in the sky as a reminder of the great truths of His Word. The constellation Virgo reminds us of the virgin birth of our Savior, Aquarius of the Great Flood of Noah, Leo of the conquering power of the Lion of the Tribe of Judah, and so forth. There have been many books written on this subject that you may be interested in.

"In the meantime," said Captain Venture, "I guess we need to get back to some of the final points of our briefing outline.

THIS IS A COMPUTER IMAGE OF THE GREAT WALL. WHITE DOTS SHOW GALAXIES (BETWEEN ARROWS) IN A THIN SHEET. EARTH LIES AT THE POINT. THE "BIG BANG" THEORY OF EVOLUTION WOULD PREDICT SMALL EVOLVING GALAXIES IN THE OUTER REACHES OF SPACE. CREATION SCIENTISTS WOULD EXPECT THE FULLY DEVELOPED GALAXIES THAT WE SEE IN THIS PICTURE. IT SEEMS THAT THE EVOLUTIONISTS HAVE A PROBLEM.

Earth

"You probably have heard a lot about the Big Bang Theory. It is now being abandoned by a great number of scientists. One of the reasons is that fully developed galaxies have been discovered at the edge of space as we know it."

"Why would that make a difference, Captain?"

"If the Big Bang Theory is true, then the galax[...]
the edge of space should be just forming.
what we see. What we see is a fully form[...]
ally complete universe. And this is only [...]

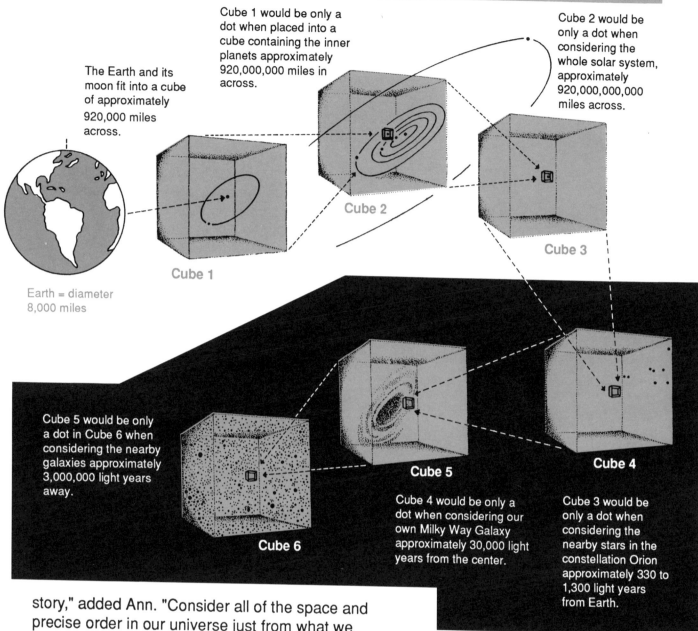

The Earth and its moon fit into a cube of approximately 920,000 miles across.

Cube 1 would be only a dot when placed into a cube containing the inner planets approximately 920,000,000 miles in across.

Cube 2 would be only a dot when considering the whole solar system, approximately 920,000,000,000 miles across.

Earth = diameter 8,000 miles

Cube 1

Cube 2

Cube 3

Cube 5 would be only a dot in Cube 6 when considering the nearby galaxies approximately 3,000,000 light years away.

Cube 6

Cube 5

Cube 4

Cube 4 would be only a dot when considering our own Milky Way Galaxy approximately 30,000 light years from the center.

Cube 3 would be only a dot when considering the nearby stars in the constellation Orion approximately 330 to 1,300 light years from Earth.

story," added Ann. "Consider all of the space and precise order in our universe just from what we know now."

Jonathan added, "If it's so easy for us to see the handiwork of God in all of this, why can't evolutionary scientists see it?"

"Remember that story Jesus told about the brothers who wouldn't believe the truth, even if someone rose from the dead and went back home and told them? I believe that's the way some people are," Ann said. "When I look at these charts and the stars on the Planetarium ceiling, it seems to me to be one huge beautiful painting done by God. It seems that in spite of the scientific evidence, there are those who don't want to see God as Creator.

Imagine all of space in the known universe reduced to the small section that we occupy. According to astronomers' writings and models, it would look something like the drawing above. (All relationships given are general estimates.)

NOTICE that the black portions are estimates of size based upon light years rather than miles.

"And we've just begun to explore, Ann," said Captain Venture. "We have mapped only about 1/100,000 of the known volume of the universe; that's about the size of Rhode Island on a world map. But God's Word tells us there are as many stars in the sky as there are grains of sand on the beach — He said that long before scientists ever figured it out!

"Well, the moment has finally come! Our briefings here at the Air Force Academy are over. Tomorrow we leave for Cape Canaveral and some extensive preflight training. Our NASA jet leaves at 0400 tomorrow. Sleep well!" exclaimed the Captain.

Approximate size of Rhode Island in a world atlas.

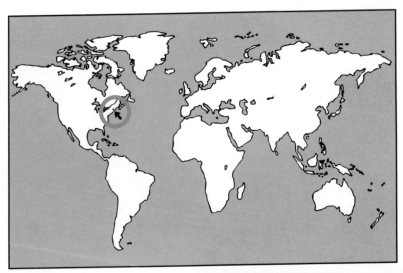

STOP FOR QUESTIONS

1. NAME A REFERENCE POINT THAT WE SHALL BE USING THAT IS MENTIONED IN SCRIPTURE.

2. WHAT IS THE ASTRONOMERS' NAME FOR THE BIG DIPPER?

3. WHERE IS THE NORTH CELESTIAL POLE?

4. SCIENTISTS HAVE MAPPED ONLY 1/100,000th OF THE VOLUME OF THE KNOWN UNIVERSE. WHAT EARTH COMPARISON DID WE MAKE FOR THIS NUMBER?

Chapter **10**
BLAST–OFF!

Time went by quickly for the young astronauts at the Cape Canaveral Center. The night before the flight, it seemed to Jonathan that he would never get to sleep. The next thing he knew, his alarm was ringing. He dressed quickly and met Ann coming out of her room. They said little as they made their way to the place where they would join Captain Venture, Major Paul, and Captain Brock.

Ann and Jonathan gave a final wave to family and friends and stepped into the NASA van that would take them to where Discovery sat, eerie and steaming in the dawn light. Their space suits were given a final check, and they entered the elevator for the ride to the top, where they entered the shuttle. Major Paul secured their seat belts and readied them for blast off, while Captain Brock went through final preflight check. Captain Venture smiled confidently at his two young companions as if to say, "Don't worry, we have it all under control."

Ann was praying as the final countdown came. "Three - Two - One - Ignition . . ."

Two rocket boosters and three powerful hydrogen/liquid oxygen engines made the spacecraft shudder as the announcement came:

"We have lift off!"

NASA photo

Jonathan could feel the pressure of acceleration. His eyeballs felt as if they were pushed to the back of his head. He wondered how Ann was doing. Ann was being squeezed against her seat as the massive space shuttle system, weighing about 2,000 tons at launch, lifted off toward the stars. They both felt the roll maneuver start at 613 feet. Just about two minutes into the launch, the spacecraft jolted as the empty rocket boosters detached themselves from the main system.

NASA photos

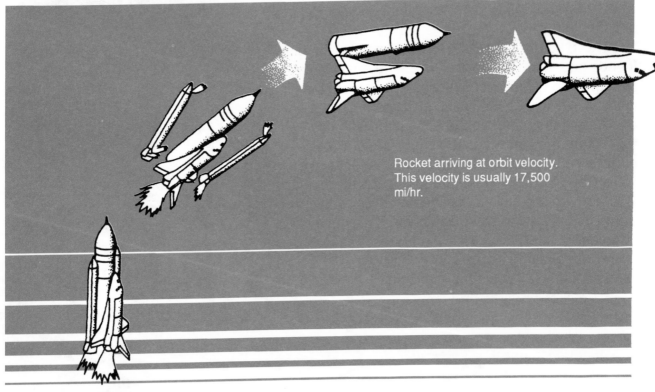

Rocket arriving at orbit velocity. This velocity is usually 17,500 mi/hr.

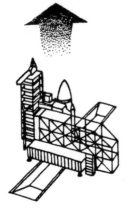

As the boosters parachuted to Earth, the voyagers waited for the next signal indicating that the propellant tank was discarded, and the space shuttle was ready for orbit. The orbiter would be kicked into an earth orbit 500 miles above the earth. With the two on-board engines, the seasoned flight crew would place the space lab in position for Captain Venture and the young scientists.

Ann was surprised at the silence of space, interrupted by a never-ending stream of communication. "Discovery, have you checked the on-board engines?" "Have you positioned the orbiter?" "What is your present vector?"

"Proceed."

Jonathan was making his own observations. "Why is space so black, and why does the earth seem so bright? I thought space would be bright!"

Captain Venture replied, "This reminds me of a very complex thing called **Olbers' Paradox**. A paradox is something which seems to be true, but which contradicts what is commonly thought. Olbers was the first to realize that if the universe were infinite, one would expect to see light everywhere. Astronomers now say that **Olbers' Paradox** is no longer a problem because dust clouds block out much of the light that would otherwise reach us.

Ann said, "Everywhere I look it makes me think of a verse in Psalms I memorized when I was little. Now it finally makes sense to me.

"It goes something like this . . . 'When I think about the heavens, the work of your hands, what is man that you are mindful of him?' Being out here in space makes me realize how small I really am!"

SOME ASTRONOMERS SAY THAT IF THE UNIVERSE HAS NO END OR BORDER THEN THERE WOULD BE AN INFINITE AMOUNT OF GALAXIES GIVING OFF AN INFINITE AMOUNT OF LIGHT. IF THIS WERE TRUE, HOW COULD THE SKY BE DARK AT NIGHT IF WE ARE ALWAYS BEING SUPPLIED WITH AN INFINITE AMOUNT OF LIGHT? (OLBERS' PARADOX)

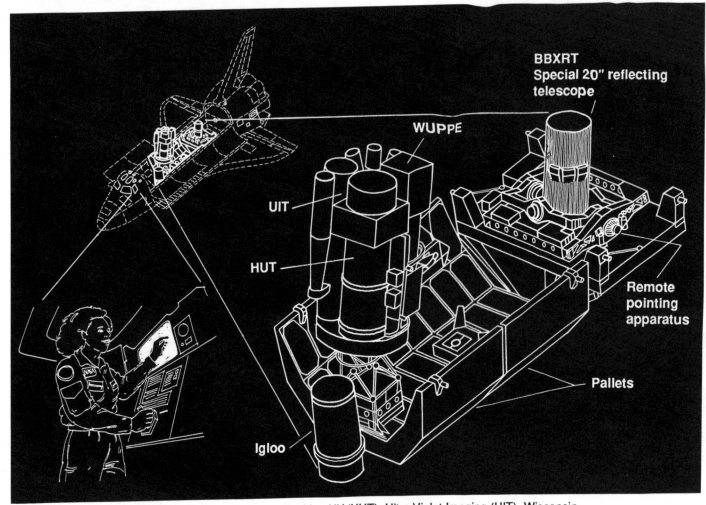

Pallets holding the three specialized telescopes: Hopkins UV (HUT), Ultra Violet Imaging (UIT), Wisconsin UV Polarimeter (WUPPE). BBXRT is modified to special (Voyage) mission. (Illustration source: NASA detail.)

PALLETS ARE PLAT-
FORMS THAT HOLD
THE TOOLS FOR THE
MISSION, IN THIS
CASE THE ASTRON-
OMY TOOLS.

"It would be very difficult for a person not to see God's hand in the order and magnitude of these created objects in the sky," said Jonathan.

"True," said Ann, "but most of them don't."

At this point, the command was given to open the outer cargo doors. The young astronaut team felt a surge of excitement. "Wow, this is what we came for!" exclaimed Jonathan.

The young crew prepared themselves for space. Captain Venture pressed another button. The inner cargo doors opened exposing the **astronomy pallets** to the awesomeness of black, silent space.

Captain Venture said to Ann and Jonathan as they were watching the remote screen on the flight laboratory deck, "Come over and check out the telescope. All of the telescope activities will be remotely operated from here."

Ann was taking directions from Captain Venture.
"Engage right ascension drive."

"I can't get it to work," said Ann.

Jonathan tried it. "I think it's stuck, Captain."

At first Captain Venture acted as though perhaps Ann and Jonathan weren't following instructions properly. But when he called Captain Brock over, they knew there really was a problem.

After a while, Captain Brock got on the radio, "Houston, we've got trouble with the right ascension drive."

A reassuring voice came over the intercom. "Roger, Discovery, we'll do some checking here and get back to you."

After what seemed forever to Ann and Jonathan, Houston radioed and confirmed that the problem was in the right ascension drive and had to be fixed by the astronauts themselves by entering the exposed cargo bay. This meant suiting up and attaching security lines.

Captain Venture, who was also trained to space walk, volunteered to suit up with Major Paul. "You'll need me to fix the telescope if something else goes wrong. Besides," he laughed, "Captain Brock better stay behind and fly our young scien-

NASA art

Orbiter with bays open, ready for operation.

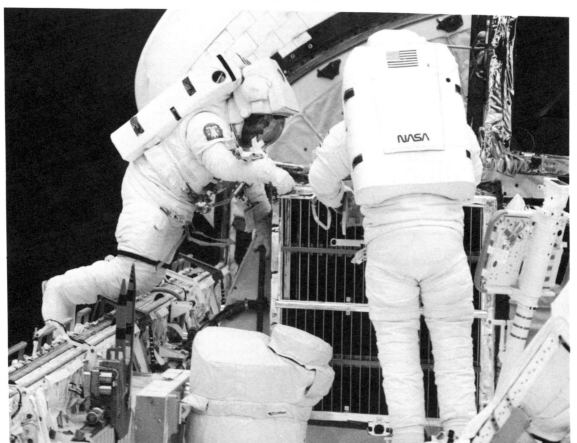

Captain Venture and Major Paul fixing the ascension drive of the telescope.

NASA photo

tists home if this turns into a long walk!"

After a lengthy preparation and more communication with mission control, Major Paul and Captain Venture entered the hatch that led to the open cargo bay. Ann and Jonathan watched intently out of the cargo bay windows as the two men entered the cargo bay to work. They seemed to move in slow motion in their bulky space suits. Ann was attracted by a bright glow off to her left. "Look, Jonathan! What's that?"

Captain Brock and Jonathan were surprised as they looked in the direction Ann indicated. Captain Brock watched intently and then said, "Looks like we have a nova star at 10 o'clock!"

"How bright do you think it is?" asked Jonathan.

"It looks like it's at 2nd magnitude now," said Ann.

After about an hour, Captain Venture and Major Paul rejoined the others. "Looks like you've found your nova, Ann. We can be sure scientists are busy tracking it, especially those at Mt. Palomar in California with their 200-inch telescope."

Jonathan could barely contain his excitement over the problem being fixed. He had been afraid that this part of the mission would have to be canceled.

Captain Venture said, "We'd better get started, we've lost valuable time repairing the telescope."

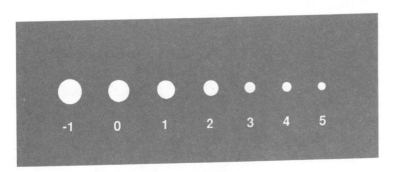

This is the scale that astronomers use to make an estimate of a star's brightness.

STOP FOR QUESTIONS

1. WHAT "PARADOX" IS SUPPOSED TO GIVE US A REASON FOR THE BLACKNESS IN SPACE?

2. WHAT IS THE ASTRONOMY PALLET ON THE SPACECRAFT USED FOR?

3. WHAT MAGNITUDE OF STAR SHOULD THE NEW SPACE TELESCOPE SEE?

Chapter **11**
FACING OUR OBJECTIVE

Captain Venture said, "As planned, we will set our **guidance optical sensors** on the region of the constellation Orion. These are special sensors on our telescope that track the stars. Remember, since our space craft is moving, the telescope has to keep moving, too."

Jonathan said, "I read that the constellation Orion contains very bright as well as very dim stars."

"That is only a small part of the Orion story," responded the Captain. "Orion contains many very beautiful **nebulae**. We will be studying some of these,

GUIDANCE OPTICAL SENSORS —THESE ARE SPECIAL SENSORS THAT HAVE BEEN BUILT INTO OUR TELESCOPE THAT WILL TRACK THE STARS. REMEMBER OUR SPACE CRAFT IS MOVING AND THE TELESCOPE HAS TO KEEP MOVING, TOO.

NEBULAE- CLOUDS OF INTERSTELLAR GAS OR DUST.

STAR CLUSTERS — STARS THAT APPEAR TO BE IN GROUPS IN SPACE.

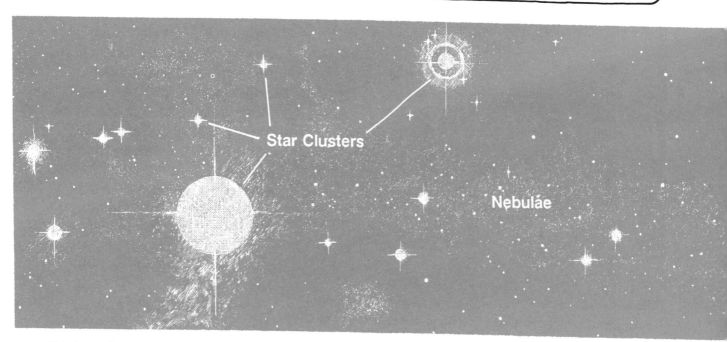

Nebulae and star clusters would appear something like this in a very close telescopic view.

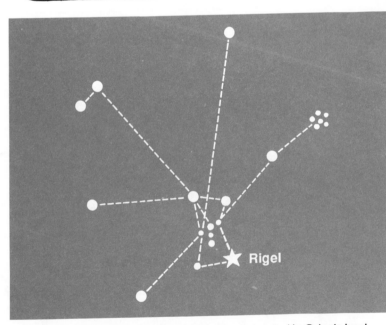

Betelgeuse, in the constellation Orion. This is the alpha star.

THE TERM ALPHA (α), BETA (β), AND GAMMA (γ) STARS USUALLY, BUT NOT ALWAYS, REFER TO A STAR'S APPARENT BRIGHTNESS IN A CONSTELLATION.

but first, we want to see what the **stars** and **star clusters** in the constellation Orion have to offer. Let's look at the star **Betelgeuse** (Beetle-juice or beh-tel-jooz).

"**Betelgeuse** is what is known as the Alpha star in the constellation Orion. Astronomers use the Greek alphabet to locate stars in the various constellations. This star is called the Great Red Giant and is actually many times bigger than our own sun. It is classified as a Super Giant.

"Remember," said Captain Venture, "brightest doesn't always mean hottest. Although **Betelgeuse** in Orion is brighter to the eye than any other star in the constellation, it is not the hottest."

"That's hard to understand," said Ann, "because I always think of something very bright as being very hot."

"That's not always true, Ann,"

Rigel, the hottest star in Orion. This star is located in Orion's heel.

THE GREEK ALPHABET

α	ALPHA	η	ETA	ν	NU	τ	TAU
β	BETA	θ	THETA	ξ	XI	υ	UPSILON
γ	GAMMA	ι	IOTA	ο	OMICRON	φ	PHI
δ	DELTA	κ	KAPPA	π	PI	χ	CHI
ε	EPSILON	λ	LAMBDA	ρ	RHO	ψ	PSI
ζ	ZETA	μ	MU	σ	SIGMA	ω	OMEGA

Greek alphabet letters used by scientists to classify stars in a constellation.

said Captain Venture. "Even though Betelgeuse is brighter to the eye, its color is reddish. Rigel (ry-gel), which is in Orion's heel, is much hotter, and appears bluish-white."

Ann said, "I remember an experiment done by German scientists. The heated object changed from red to white to bluish-white when it was the hottest."

"Hey, that's right, Ann! If those scientists could see us now, what would they think?"

> THIS IS ANOTHER THING ABOUT CONSTELLATIONS THAT YOU WILL WANT TO KNOW. THE GREEK LETTERING HAS MORE TO DO WITH THE IMPORTANCE OF A STAR IN A CONSTELLATION THAN ANYTHING ELSE.

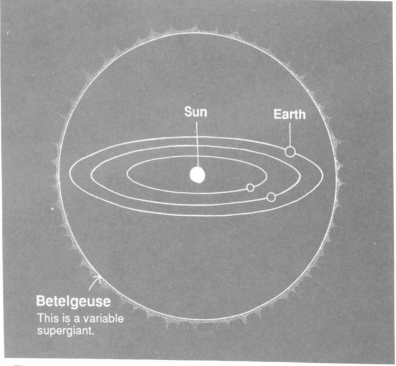

The red supergiant Betelgeuse is at least 200 times the diameter of the sun. Notice the size of Betelgeuse compared to the Earth's orbit.

Their nervousness had lessened and the two young scientists began to realize their planetarium had been replaced by the real thing.

Captain Venture had some more to add on this subject.

He commented, "Another interesting point about **Betelgeuse** is the fact that it is a **variable star**.

"Rigel is a zero magnitude star and a double star. When we look at stars such as Rigel, they seem to be just one point of light, but in reality they are two or more stars circling around a single point. Remember, we discussed this in our briefing."

Jonathan said, "I have read that when one of the stars in a double star system gets in front of the brightest star, it blocks the light from the star behind so that it appears that the brightness changes."

Ann commented, "There are so many important terms to know when we talk about stars and constellations."

"It does get kind of confusing," said Jonathan. "But I think it's fun to speak astronomers' language.

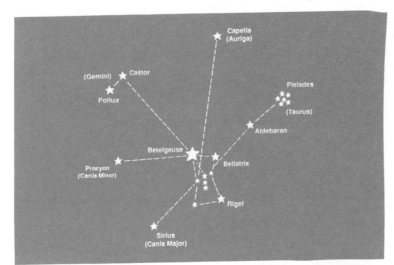

Showing the relationship of Betelgeuse to other stars in Constellation Orion.

STOP FOR QUESTIONS

1. WHAT CONSTELLATION IS OUR FIRST OBJECTIVE?

2. WHAT IS THE ALPHA STAR IN ORION?

3. NAME A SUPERGIANT STAR IN ORION.

4. WHAT IS THE HOTTEST STAR IN ORION?

NOTICE THAT KELVIN AND CENTIGRADE DIVISIONS ARE THE SAME EXCEPT THAT K STARTS WITH AB- SOLUTE ZERO.

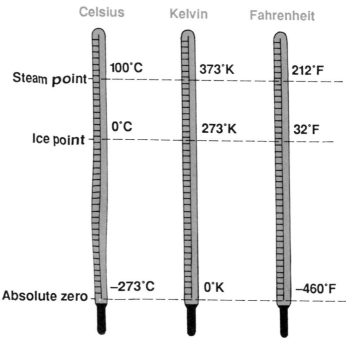

	Celsius	Kelvin	Fahrenheit
Steam point	100°C	373°K	212°F
Ice point	0°C	273°K	32°F
Absolute zero	−273°C	0°K	−460°F

Chapter **12**

STARS: WHAT ARE THEY MADE OF?

Ann and Jonathan examined the light coming from **Betelgeuse** through the spectroscope. Ann asked Captain Venture, "Do scientists know the temperature of this star?"

"Betelgeuse has a temperature that ranges from 3000° to 3500° on the **Kelvin** scale. This star shows strong **spectral lines** that indicate it has a great abundance of the compound titanium oxide.

"On the other hand," continued the Captain, "**Rigel**'s temperature is 11,000° to 25,000° Kelvin. Its spectral lines indicate that **helium** is abundant. It is very different from our own sun, with a temperature of 5000° to 6000° Kelvin, and with spectral lines that indicate an abundance of the element **calcium**."

Ann said, "Spectroanalysis is a pretty awesome thing!"

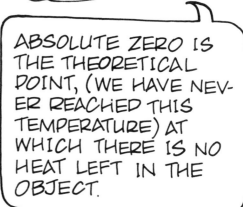

ABSOLUTE ZERO IS THE THEORETICAL POINT, (WE HAVE NEVER REACHED THIS TEMPERATURE) AT WHICH THERE IS NO HEAT LEFT IN THE OBJECT.

Captain Venture said, "We can also tell from spectroanalysis that not all stars burn up the same amount of fuel. Now, don't misunderstand me, about 99% of all stars are made up of hydrogen and helium gas, but they also burn other elements."

"That's a good way to say it, Jonathan. Each star is different from another. The Bible teaches this. It says one star differs from another star in glory."

Ann said, "I'm learning that whenever the Bible talks about science, it always seems to be correct, yet it was written long before scientists made their observations."

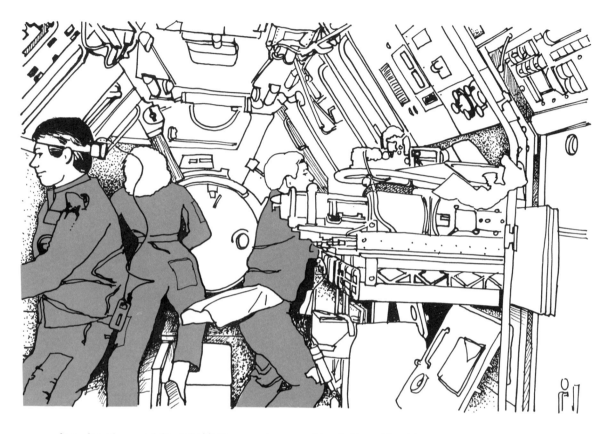

Ann, Jonathan and Captain Venture are busy working in the orbiter laboratory.

"That's right, Ann," said Captain Venture. "Most stars are found to contain hydrogen and helium gas, but they also differ in many other ways, including their density.

"Some stars are super dense and are called **neutron stars** and **white dwarfs**."

Jonathan said, "I've heard about these. Did you know if you squeezed all the Great Lakes together so that their density equaled that of a neutron star, all the water in those lakes would fit in a kitchen sink!"

"That's a lot of water to fit in a kitchen sink," Ann said a little skeptically.

"It's true," said Captain Venture.

"It would take some sink to hold that!" laughed Ann.

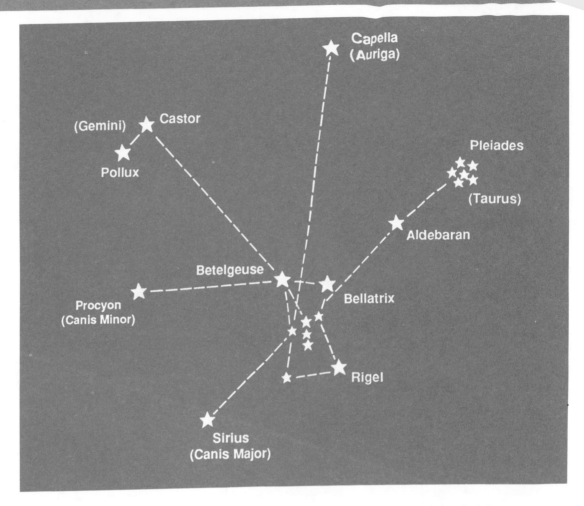

Capella
(Auriga)

(Gemini) Castor

Pollux

Pleiades

(Taurus)

Aldebaran

Betelgeuse

Bellatrix

Procyon
(Canis Minor)

Rigel

Sirius
(Canis Major)

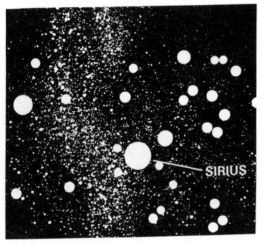

Sirius, the Dog Star

"Now let's turn the telescope toward the brightest star in the sky," said Captain Venture. "It's called **Sirius**, the **Dog Star**."

Ann found Sirius without any trouble because she had done her homework. She knew it was in a straight line downward from what is known as **Orion's Belt**.

When Captain Venture analyzed the spectrum of Sirius, he found that its temperature was between 7500° and 11,000° Kelvin. Also, he noted that it was a **binary star**.

"Captain Venture," said Ann, "Sirius has always looked like one point of light to me. I never thought it would be two stars circling each other."

"Another interesting thing about Sirius, Ann, is that the spectrograph has shown that it is burning hydrogen and perhaps even calcium and helium for fuel."

Jonathan said, "Can you believe how much information we can get from the spectrum of a star?"

"Actually," Captain Venture said, "there's a whole group of star classifications based just on their spectra."

Captain Venture showed Jonathan and Ann a spectrum chart and asked, "Who knows what a **mnemonic** is?"

"I remember!" said Jonathan with a big grin. "It's a memory device!"

"Very good, Jonathan. We have one so you both can remember star classifications. It's 'O.h B.e A. F.ine G.irl, K.iss M.e'."

Ann wrinkled up her nose at the Captain and Jonathan. "I don't think I'd be a fine girl just because I kissed anyone—but it is a good way to remember!"

THIS CHART WAS ORIGINALLY BASED UPON THE SPECTRAL LINES OF HYDROGEN GAS. AT THE TIME, ASTRONOMERS DIDN'T KNOW THAT HYDROGEN WAS NOT ALWAYS THE HOTTEST BURNING GAS. THIS INFORMATION CAME LATER, SO YOU CAN SEE WHY THE LETTERS BECAME MIXED UP.

STAR	APPROXIMATE TEMPERATURE	COLOR	COLOR SPECTRAL TYPE	
VEGA	22,050°F	BLUE-WHITE	A	BLUE
SIRIUS	20,650°F	BLUE-WHITE	A	BLUE-WHITE
CANOPUS	15,850°F	WHITE	F	WHITE
PROCYON	12,650°F	YELLOW-WHITE	F	WHITE-YELLOW
CAPELLA	11,050°F	YELLOWISH	G	YELLOW
THE SUN	10,950°F	YELLOWISH	G	YELLOW
ARCTURUS	8,450°F	ORANGE	K	ORANGE
ANTARES	5,850°F	REDDISH	M	RED

Most of the stars can be classified into the seven basic types:
O B A F G K M

CAN YOU SEE THE RELATIONSHIP BETWEEN THE TEMPERATURE OF A STAR ON THIS CHART AND ITS COLOR?

Jonathan asked, "Can we talk about black holes? They're a hot item in astronomy class!"

"Sure," answered the Captain. "However, most everything we know about black holes is still theory."

"Do they exist?" asked Ann.

"Most astronomers think they do exist," said Captain Venture. "They even classify them as they do stars. But, of course, they can't see them. They're very complex. The mass in a black hole is said to be so great that light cannot escape."

"That's why they're called 'black holes,' right?" asked Jonathan.

"At any rate, it's still theory," said the Captain.

This is a scientist's idea of what a black hole might look like.

"Captain, why do astronomers classify objects they can't see?" asked Jonathan. "That doesn't seem very scientific to me."

"Jonathan, there is much we don't know about space, but if we use the minds God gave us, we can make reasonable assumptions."

"That's right," said Ann. "I think God wants us to use our brains the best we can to explore the things He has made."

"There is so much more to learn about the stars, it boggles my mind," said Jonathan. "I guess God knew when He created everything that someday there would be people like us to wonder about the awesome things He has put in space!"

STOP FOR QUESTIONS

1. NAME THREE TEMPERATURE SCALES

2. FROM THE STARS MENTIONED IN OUR STORY, NAME TWO THAT BURN CALCIUM, IN THEIR CORE.

3. WHAT STAR IS CALLED THE DOG STAR?

4. WHAT MNEMONIC GIVES ALL THE SPECTRUM LETTERS IN THE SPECTRUM CHART?

Chapter **13**

TURNING OUR TELESCOPES ON THE NEBULAE

Captain Venture said, "Let's turn the telescope towards Barnard's Loop, that large hazy mass in the sky north of Orion's belt on your star chart. **Barnard's Loop** is a large shell of hydrogen gas that surrounds part of Orion."

Ann said, "And the spectrograph gave us this information?"

"That's correct, Ann," said the Captain. "A spectroanalysis of the Loop clearly indicates it is a mass of hydrogen gas. Actually, this object is very hard to see through Earth's haze, but we have little trouble seeing it from our orbiting station."

Ann turned the telescope so she and Jonathan could see more of the sky.

"Now I know why agnostics say, 'In the beginning hydrogen . . .' There's a lot of it out there!" commented Jonathan.

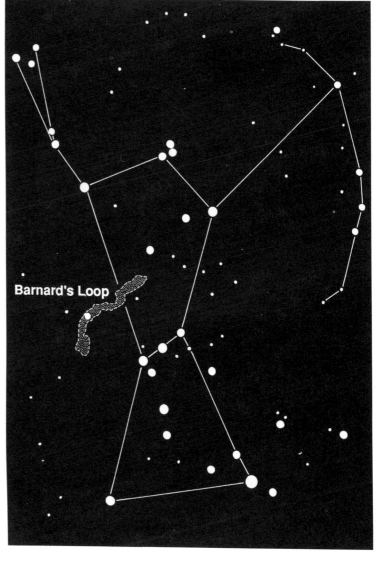

Barnard's Loop in the constellation Orion.

Captain Venture responded, "Truth is, that is one of the most unscientific statements an astronomer could ever make. 'In the beginning, God' is far more in keeping with scientific truth. Hydrogen gas alone could never have produced our complex universe, no matter how much time we gave it!"

Captain Venture began preparations to photograph Barnard's Loop. "From this vantage point, we will be able to bring back some good clear photographs to our Earth lab.

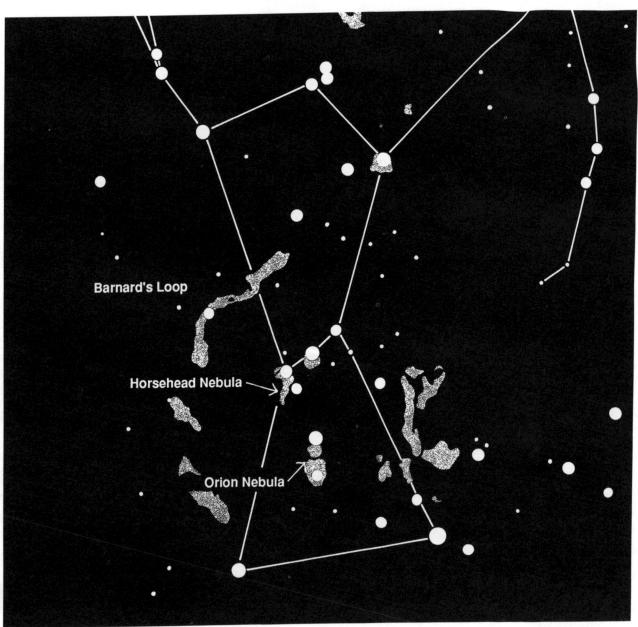

Horsehead Nebula

Star Charts

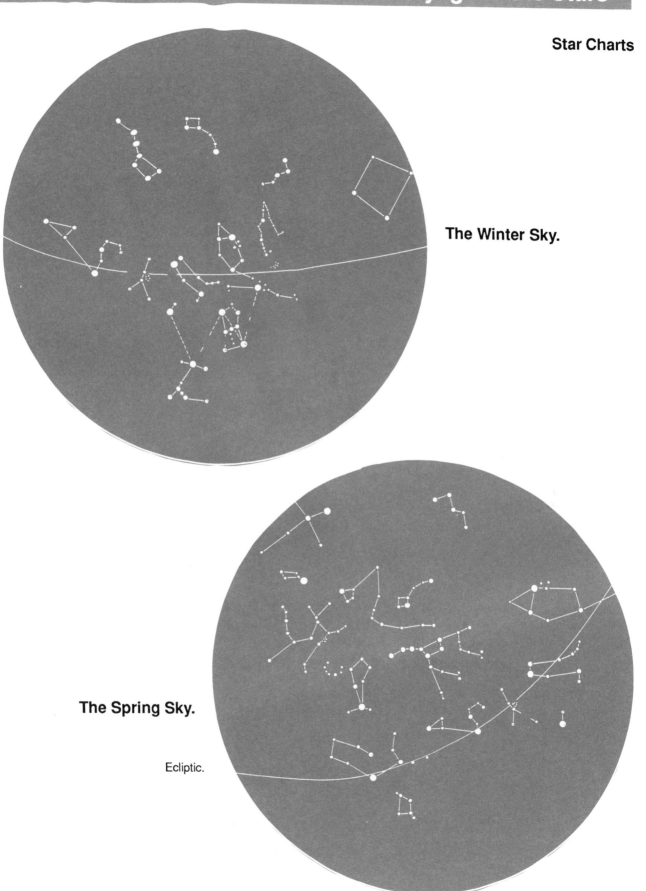

The Winter Sky.

The Spring Sky.

Ecliptic.

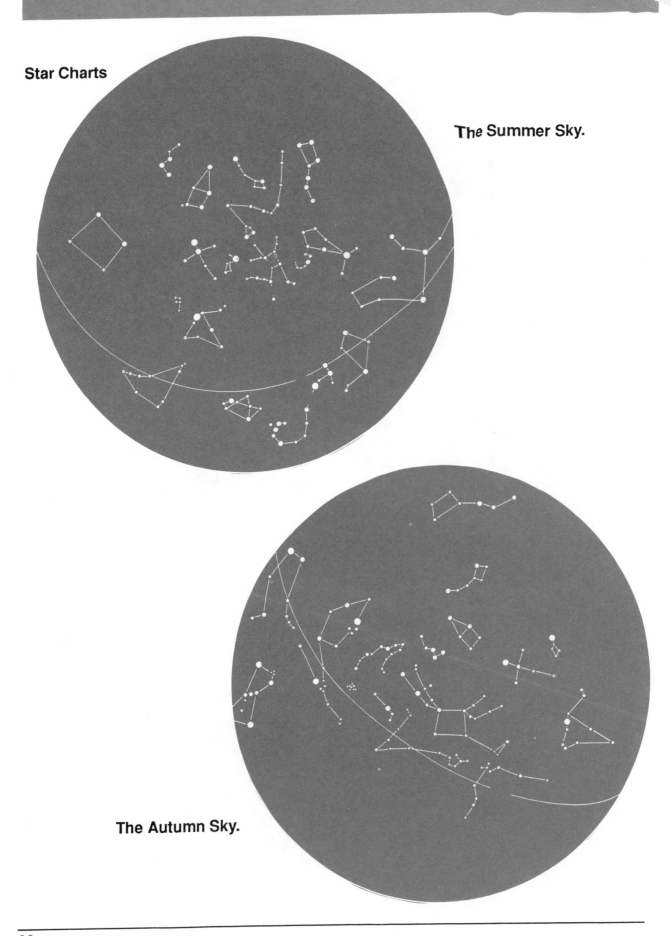

Star Charts

The Summer Sky.

The Autumn Sky.

"Usually it takes a long photographic exposure of this area from Earth in order to see the Loop clearly."

"We won't have any trouble from here!" said Jonathan.

The telescope was equipped with a high-speed camera lens. After setting it to run automatically, the team turned their attention to the next objective.

Ann said, "There are so many things to see here!"

"You're right, Ann," said Jonathan, "and this is just one area of the sky!"

"Now you know why we picked Orion as our primary objective for this voyage," said Captain Venture. "For instance, look at this chart. How many interesting constellations can you find using Orion as a reference point?"

Ann pointed: "There, just above Orion, are the Gemini Twins! What are their names?"

"**Castor** and **Pollux**," said Captain Venture. "Their names come from the Greek legend. I believe, how-

Pleiades in extended photographic exposure.

THERE ARE FOUR BRIGHT STARS CALLED TRAPEZIUM, THREE OF THE STARS WITH MAGNITUDES 5.1, 6.7 AND 7.9. THESE ARE THE STARS THAT LIGHT UP THE NEBULA.

ever, as we talked about before, that God placed them in the heavens as a testimony to His truth."

"According to the chart," said Jonathan, "Castor is the Alpha star and Pollux is the Beta star. That doesn't seem right. Castor is a fainter 2nd-magnitude star, and Pollux is a 1st-magnitude star. Aren't they just turned around?

"Remember, Jonathan," said the Captain, "the Greek letters are not always assigned on the basis of brightness, but on the basis of what the astronomers consider their importance in the constellation."

The next objective on their list was to examine the **Orion Nebula**.

Captain Venture exclaimed suddenly, "This area of the sky is a photographic feast!"

When the Orion Nebula (sometimes called the **Great Nebula**) appeared on the remote screen of the telescope, there was an unusual silence as the viewers held their breath in wonder.

Before their eyes was a magnificent, luminous cloud. "The brightness and color take my breath away!" Ann exclaimed.

Captain Venture said, "Sometimes this nebula is referred to as the Orion Nebula, but when viewed from the space shuttle, the word Great Nebula seems more fitting."

"Seeing photographs is one thing," said Jonathan, "but seeing something so awesome from out here is, well, it's . . . 'AWESOME'!"

"Are you ready for this next view?" asked Captain Venture as he swung the telescope toward the **Horsehead Nebula** in the belt of Orion.

Ann said, "It just doesn't seem possible for such beautiful things to just hang in space, waiting for us to discover them, and yet, God has known about them all along."

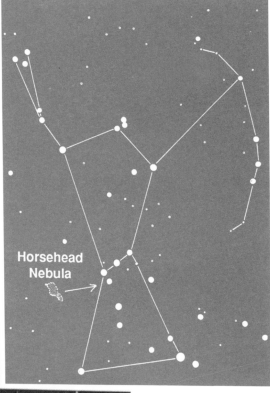

Horsehead
Nebula

The Horsehead Nebula in the Constellation Orion.

The Trapezium, lighting up the nebula.

Jonathan helped Captain Venture lock the sensors on the area in the far left of Orion's belt where they would see the Horsehead Nebula. Jonathan saw the picture come up on the remote (CRT) screen, then whistled and exclaimed, "Ann! Look!"

After a moment or two the exclamations subsided and Captain Venture said, "That's the Horsehead Nebula, and it is lit by a double star. The outline of the horse is caused by light-absorbing gases. We are just now beginning to understand how this nebula is formed; it's a great testimony to the awesome beauty God has put into His universe.

STOP FOR QUESTIONS

1. WHERE CAN WE FIND BARNARD'S LOOP?

2. WHAT IS ANOTHER NAME FOR THE ORION NEBULA?

3. WHAT IS A NEBULA?

4. WHAT IS A TRAPEZIUM?

Chapter **14**

THE GALAXIES: WONDER OF WONDERS

NEBULAE — GAS AND DUST PARTICLES AROUND THE STARS AND GALAXIES.

"Captain Venture, who will use our photographs?" asked Ann.

"Depending upon their quality, I think they could be used in books or schools, or a number of places!"

"I would like to have some copies to take back to show my friends at school."

"Me, too!" said Jonathan.

"In that case, you'll like the photographs we take today," said the Captain. "Let's locate the **Magellanic Clouds**."

The Milky Way Galaxy.

A spiral galaxy.

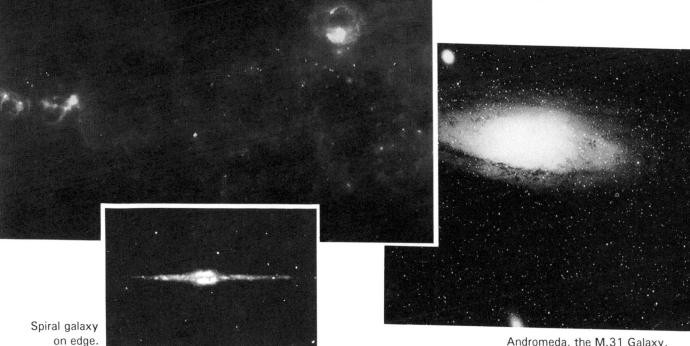

Spiral galaxy on edge.

Andromeda, the M.31 Galaxy.

Elliptical   Spiral   Irregular

Galaxies are classified by their shapes.
These are some of the various shapes
we find in our universe.

Ann and Jonathan fixed the telescope on the
Constellation **Hydrus** and moved the telescope west
toward the constellation **Tucana**. They soon located
the galaxies they were looking for.

Captain Venture explained, "The Large and Small
Magellanic Clouds are two of the closest to our own
galaxy, the **Milky Way**. They get their names from
being first seen by Magellan's crew."

"We have the advantage of *sailing* around
the world a lot quicker than Magellan did!"
said Ann.

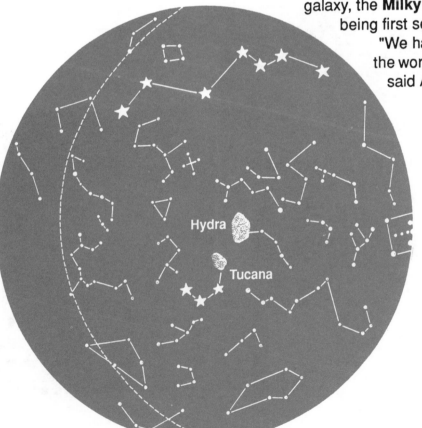

The Constellations Hydrus
and Tucana the Toucan.

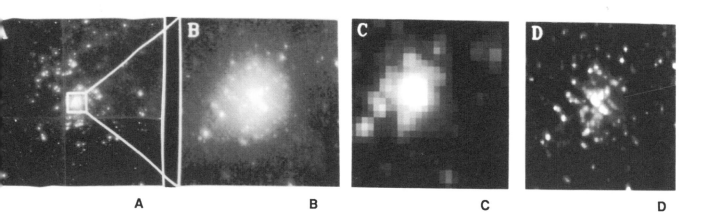

This is a Hubble Telescope photograph series showing a small cluster (**A**) of stars in the Large Magellanic Cloud Galaxy. Notice how large and clear the cluster is in the enlarged photograph (**B**). In photo (**D**) you can see how a computer can clear up the image for sharp focus. Compare all of this with the photograph taken from a ground telescope (**C**) in Chile.

"The **Large Magellanic Cloud** covers a distance of at least 20,000 light years. We estimate that it contains as many as 30 billion stars," said the Captain.

"No wonder it is visible from the Earth," said Jonathan, "even without a telescope!"

"I'm happy we have a wide field lens for the telescope because this cloud, sometimes called a Magellanic Stream, would be difficult to study otherwise. Just think, a cloud of gas stretching over much of the sky! Here are some recent Hubble photographs of that area of the sky," said Captain Venture.

The Andromeda Galaxy, found in the constellation Andromeda.

> ANDROMEDA IS SAID TO BE TWO MILLION LIGHT YEARS AWAY. THIS IS THE SPIRAL GALAXY THAT GAVE US THE IDEA ABOUT OUR OWN MILKY WAY GALAXY.

"Next, let's take a look at the **Andromeda Galaxy**, which is in the constellation. **Andromeda**

"As time went on, new telescopes, like the 40" refractor at Yerkes Observatory, began to take very long exposures of the sky. This telescope was the first to reveal the spiral nature of the Andromeda Galaxy. Actually, M 31 looks much like our own Milky Way because of its disk-like shape."

Ann asked, "Why is it called M 31, Captain?"

Captain Venture decided to take a few moments and review the astronomer's numbering systems.

"In 1784, a French scientist named Charles Messier gave numbers to various star clusters in the sky. He did this so they wouldn't be mistaken for comets. In all, he numbered 103 objects. These were called **Messier numbers**.

"Later in history," continued Captain Venture, "another astronomer developed his own numbering system called the New General Catalog (NGC). The Andromeda Galaxy actually has two numbers, M.31 and NGC 224." One of these indicates a Messier number and the other the New General Catalogue number."

"It's easy to get mixed up in astronomers' numbers, isn't it?" asked Ann.

"Well, I'm more interested in looking at Andromeda than figuring out its number!" said Jonathan.

Jonathan pointed the remote controls in the direction of Andromeda. "There it is!"

Look at it on the telescope screen, Ann."

"What a sight! Let's take some pictures!"

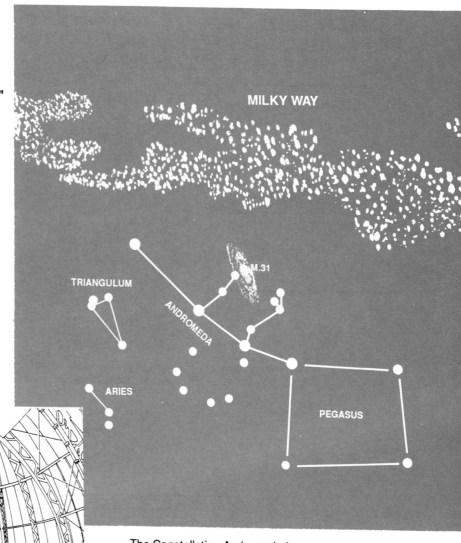

The Constellation <u>Andromeda</u> is connected to the Constellation Pegasus (The Horse) by the star Alpha Andromedae. Notice the location of the Andromeda Galaxy (M-31) in the constellation Andromeda.

MESSIER=M

NEW GENERAL CAT-
ALOGUE = NGC

Refractor telescope similar to the one found at "Yerkes" Observatory in Williams Bay, Wisconsin.

> BY APPLYING THE LAWS OF PHYSICS, SCIENTISTS CAN LEARN MUCH. REMEMBER, THESE ARE LAWS OF ORDER.

"There's another interesting point about our own galaxy. In 1917, the well known astronomer Harlow Shapley looked toward the constellation Sagittarius and saw what appeared to be a cluster of stars like a giant bubble in the sky. He reasoned this was the center of the Milky Way. We still think this is true today."

Jonathan was impressed that an astronomer-scientist could come up with such an idea.

> ANDROMEDA IS ROUGHLY DOUBLE THE SIZE OF OUR OWN MILKY WAY GALAXY.

Milky Way Galaxy as it might look if we were out in space looking at it. Notice that our little planet Earth would be way out at the edge of the galaxy.

STOP FOR QUESTIONS

1. NAME THREE CLASSES OF GALAXIES.

2. WHAT IS THE CONSTELLATION SAGITTARIUS' COMMON NAME?

3. WHAT IS A MESSIER NUMBER?

4. WHAT DOES NGC MEAN?

Chapter **15**
GOING HOME

Discovery had been in orbit for seven days and it was time to return to Earth.

"We have an excellent weather window," said Major Paul, "and we'll be landing at Edwards Air Force Base in California."

The cargo bays were closed, and the team went through the necessary procedures and made themselves ready for re-entry.

Ann and Jonathan were ready to go home. They had so much to share with their parents and friends at school about the stars they had seen, the telescope they had used, and especially the unexpected nova.

NASA photo

> *"And there shall be no more curse: but the throne of God and of the Lamb shall be in it; and His servants shall serve Him."*
>
> (Revelation 22:3 KJV)

> *"Space travel will be commonplace, of course, in that day..."*
>
> (Henry M. Morris, THE REVELATION RECORD)

Ann took a last look toward space and then settled down in her seat to prepare for the descent of Discovery to the desert floor of California.

She looked toward the earth and said, "It seems like a long time since we were sitting in the Planetarium looking at the maps and getting ready for this trip. Captain Venture, do you remember when you said that sometimes the unexpected leads to new discoveries?"

"Yes, I do," said the Captain. "Did anything unexpected happen to you on this trip?"

"Well," said Ann, "the telescope broke down."

"Yeah," said Jonathan, "I was afraid that the unexpected would lead to no discovery, rather than a new discovery."

"I don't know if this is a new discovery," said Ann, "but it did make me think of how everything wears out . . . and not just man-made telescopes, but even the nova made me think of how things decay."

"In fact," said Jonathan, "lots of things we saw are like that. There must be a tremendous amount of energy being used up by the stars."

"That's true," said Captain Venture, "and we can make certain assumptions about the stars and even about their chemical reactions. But because we can't examine a star in a laboratory, it's difficult for us to be absolutely certain about our conclusions."

Ann thought, " I wonder what eternity will be like? Are we being prepared to explore God's creation in heaven? Will we find out about these things for certain?"

Jonathan commented, "It may be that what the Bible has taught us about stars being different from one another, in even more ways, will be discovered by scientists in our lifetime. Perhaps we will be explorers busy for all eternity. I am looking forward to that.

"Speaking of looking forward to things," said Jonathan, "I can't wait to get home and tell my friends about this mission!"

Major Paul said, "We are approaching the Earth's atmosphere. We may experience some rough spots along the way, but don't worry. You might also be interested in watching the glow because of the great increase in temperature as we fall through the atmosphere." At that moment, Ann exclaimed, "Hey! Look at the re-entry glow out the window! Isn't that exciting?"

Captain Brock and Major Paul executed a flawless landing amid the cheers of onlookers. The first teens in space appeared in the doorway waving to family and friends.

While the reporters and others were still taking pictures, Captain Venture said, "Well, Ann, Jonathan, I want to thank you for such an outstanding job. I couldn't ask for a better young scientist team. You may be interested to know that we are considering another voyage in the near future. You can be sure that if and when I get my orders, I'll be calling you."

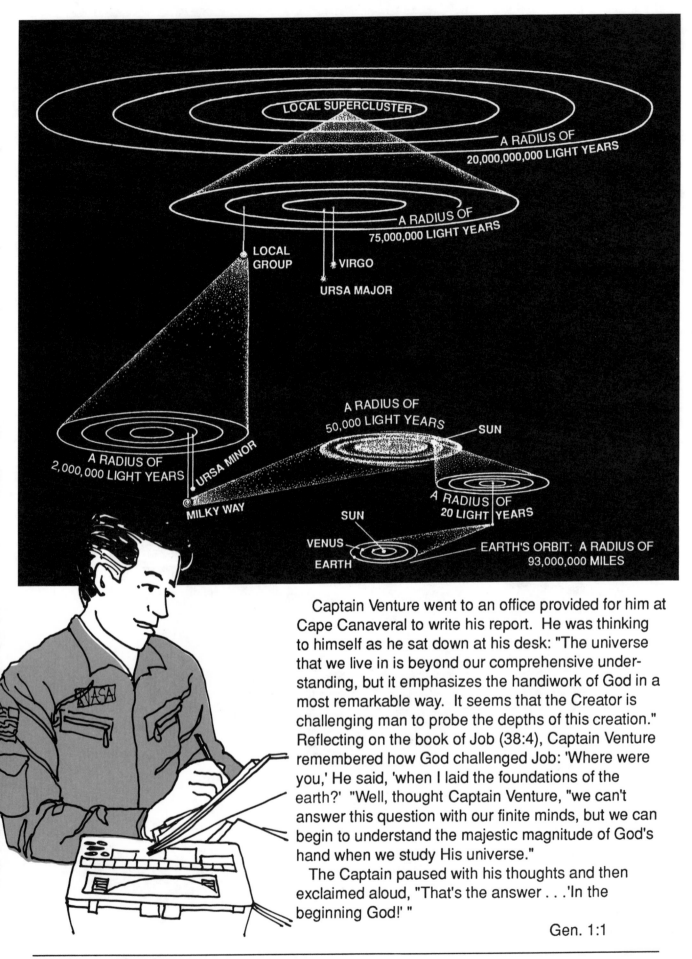

Captain Venture went to an office provided for him at Cape Canaveral to write his report. He was thinking to himself as he sat down at his desk: "The universe that we live in is beyond our comprehensive understanding, but it emphasizes the handiwork of God in a most remarkable way. It seems that the Creator is challenging man to probe the depths of this creation." Reflecting on the book of Job (38:4), Captain Venture remembered how God challenged Job: 'Where were you,' He said, 'when I laid the foundations of the earth?' "Well, thought Captain Venture, "we can't answer this question with our finite minds, but we can begin to understand the majestic magnitude of God's hand when we study His universe."

The Captain paused with his thoughts and then exclaimed aloud, "That's the answer . . .'In the beginning God!' "

Gen. 1:1

INDEX

BIBLIOGRAPHY

1. **The Facts on File Dictionary of Astronomy**, Editor; Valerie Illingworth, Macmillan Press, Ltd., 1985.

2. Page, Williams Lou, **Ideas from Astronomy**, Addison-Wesley Publishing, Menlo Park, California, 1973.

3. Menzel, Donald H., Pasachoff, Jay M., **A Field Guide to Stars and Planets** (Peterson Field Guide Series).

4. DeYoung, Donald B., Whitcomb, John C., **The Moon; Its Creation, Form and Significance**, BMH Books, 1978.

5. **Tapes of the Night Sky**, The Astronomical Society of the Pacific.

6. Whitcomb, John C., **The Bible and Astronomy**, BMH Books, Winona Lake, Indiana, 1984.

7. Muirden, James, **The Universe**, Simon and Schuster, New York, 1987.

8. Monkhouse, Richard; Cox, John, **3-D Star Map**, Harper and Row, New York, 1989.

9. National Geographic Society, Washington, D.C., Supplement to the National Geographic, June 1983.

10. **The Rand McNally New Concise Atlas of the Universe**, Rand McNally and Company, New York, Chicago, San Francisco, 1978.

11. The Observatories of the Carnegie Institute of Washington.

12. Kaufmann, William J., III: **Universe**, second edition, W.F. Freeman and Co., New York, 1988.

13. Huffer, Charles; Trinklein, Fredrick; Bunge, Mark: **An Introduction to Astronomy**, Holt, Rinehart and Winston, Inc., 1973.

PHOTO CREDITS

GLOSSARY OF TERMS

Absolute Magnitude—A measure of the actual brightness of a star.

Absolute Zero—The point where there is no heat left in an object. This point is 0° K or -273° C.

Absorption Spectra—Dark lines in the spectrum that show absorption by certain gases.

Andromeda Constellation—A constellation in the northern hemisphere close to the constellation Pegasus.

Andromeda Galaxy—The largest of the nearby galaxies. It appears as a faint oval patch of light in the constellation Andromeda. This galaxy is roughly twice as large as our own galaxy.

Apparent Magnitude—The brightness of a star through general viewing from the earth or a space platform.

Arcturus—The alpha star in the constellation Bootes; zero magnitude star.

Astrologers—Men and women who practice astrology, a pseudo scientific practice condemned by the Bible.

Astrology—The pseudo scientific study of the stars, whereby the stars become divine predictors of events.

Astronomical Unit (AU)—The distance between the Earth and the sun, an average of 93,000,000 miles.

Barnard's Loop—A very large shell of hydrogen gas (ionized) in the constellation Orion.

Betelgeuse—The alpha star in the constellation Orion.

Binary Star System—A pair of stars that revolve around each other (having the same center of mass), and are held there by each other's gravitational attraction.

Black Hole—A theoretical collapsed star that is thought to be so dense that light cannot escape.

Bright Line Spectra—Bright lines in the spectrum that show the presence of certain elements.

Calcium—A white metallic-looking substance that is in the 20th position on the periodic chart. A common rock is made of calcium carbonate.

Carbon Dioxide—A common gas compound given off by all living systems.

Cassegrain Telescope—A popular telescope with a special focus point at the end of the telescope tube.

Castor—One of the Gemini Twins, Castor, the alpha star in the Gemini constellation.

Celestial Equator—The great circle on the celestial sphere corresponding to the projection of Earth's equator onto the sphere.

Celestial Sphere—The imaginary sphere of sight in the sky.

Centigrade—A temperature scale with freezing point at 0° and boiling point at 100°. Absolute zero is -273°.

Cepheid Variable—A very bright star that pulsates regularly.

Constellations—Star group shapes in the sky, given names such as Orion, Taurus, etc. The entire sky is divided into 88 constellations.

Coordinates—Numbers that define the position or location of a star, a spacecraft, or even where you are right now.

Dark Line Spectra—Dark lines in a continuous spectrum that show light absorption by elements in a star's atmosphere.

Declination—A coordinate system for measuring north–south positions on the celestial sphere.

Diffraction Grating—A grating that has a large number of lines per inch. When light passes through, it is separated into the spectrum of colors.

Double Star—Two stars that appear close together. These stars are bound together by gravitation.

Earth Rotation—The spin of the earth; approximately 1,000 miles an hour on the surface near the equator.

Ecliptic—The apparent yearly path of the sun.

Elliptical—An oblong shape; technically, a cone section that is cut through with a plane.

Escape Velocity—The velocity that any object has to move to escape the Earth's gravitational field (25,000 mi/hr) from a low Earth orbit.

Extrapolate—Projecting scientific data beyond the known information.

Fahrenheit—A temperature scale with 32° freezing point of water, 212° boiling point of water, and -460° absolute zero.

Fraunhofer Lines—Absorption lines in the sun's spectrum; discovered by Joseph von Fraunhofer.

Galaxies—A large group of stars, nebulae, and interstellar gas and dust. Our own Milky Way Galaxy is an example.

Gemini Twins—One of the Zodiac constellations. Greek legend says the god Zeus placed Pollux next to Castor, his half-brother, in the sky.

Great Nebula—Sometimes called the Orion Nebula, it is found near Orion's sword in the constellation Orion.

Great Red Giant—A common term for the Alpha Star in Orion called Betelgeuse.

Greek Alphabet in Astronomy—The alphabet—alpha, beta, gamma, etc. — used to classify stars by their brightness in a constellation.

Gyrocompass—A compass that uses a gyroscope instead of a magnetic needle for direction.

Helium—A very light inert gas. This gas does not naturally combine with other atoms; it is one of the inert gases. Helium is not an explosive gas.

Horsehead Nebula—A dark cloud of gas and cosmic dust that blocks out the light of very bright stars. The image of a horse head is seen as a silhouette.

Hubble Space Telescope—A high-tech telescope that now orbits the Earth at 370 miles. The Hubble Space Telescope will send back star images about 50 times more clear than the best Earth telescope.

Hydra—The largest constellation in the sky, called the sea serpent.

Hydrogen—The lightest gas known, it burns at high temperatures and explodes in the presence of heat and oxygen.

Hyperbolic—An oblong shape. Technically, a curve formed by cutting a circular cone with a plane steeper than the sides of the cone.

Ionosphere—A layer of the Earth's atmosphere that has many ionized atoms in it. There are three layers (D, E, F), all of which can interfere with radio waves.

Kelvin—A temperature scale with 273° freezing point of water, 373 boiling point of water, and 0 absolute zero.

Latitude Grid—A grid that has many latitude lines used on a circular globe.

Light Year—The distance that light travels in one year, about six trillion miles.

Longitude Grid—A grid that has many longitude lines used on a circular globe.

Luminosity—The actual brightness of a star; absolute magnitude.

Magellanic Clouds—The Small Magellanic Cloud is found in the constellation Tucana, the Toucan; the Large Magellanic Cloud is in Dorado.

Magnitude—The amount of light received from a star.

Magnitude Chart—A chart that shows relative brightness of stars by showing them as larger and smaller circular dots.

Maksutov Telescope—A compact telescope with a special correcting plate built into it.

Mass—The amount of matter in a body.

Messier Numbers—Numbers given to objects in the sky in the 18th century by French scientist Charles Messier.

Meteorite—A mass of stone or metal that has reached the earth from outer space. A fallen meteoroid.

Military Clock—A 24-hour clock, as opposed to our standard 12-hour clock.

Milky Way Galaxy—Our own galaxy, easily seen on a clear night, looking along the disc.

Mnemonic—A word memory system.

NASA—National Aeronautics and Space Administration.

Debula—A cloud of interstellar gas and dust.

Neutron Star—A very dense (compact) star, composed almost entirely of neutrons.

NGC (New General Catalogue) Numbers—A listing of celestial objects. This listing is more current than Messier numbers.

North Celestial Pole—A point on the celestial sphere directly above the north pole and about 1 degree from the star Polaris.

Nova Star—A star that seems to explode to many times its original brightness and then fades back to its original state.

Olber's Paradox—An explanation for space being so black. This is also a theory for space being limited in size.

Optical Sensors—These are fine guidance sensors used to track stars and other objects.

Orbit—The closed path that an object follows around a gravitational object or point. The moon orbits the Earth. Satellites orbit the Earth.

Orion—A very obvious constellation that lies on the celestial equator, close to the Milky Way. Orion can be seen in its entirety from most parts of the Earth.

Orion's Belt—Composed of three remote 2nd-magnitude stars.

Orion Nebula—One of the brightest nebula in the sky. Found in the center of Orion's sword, it is also known as the Great Nebula.

Oxygen—21% of the gas in the Earth's atmosphere. A necessity of life for most plants and animals.

Pallets—Platforms attached to the cargo bay of a space vehicle for holding scientific experiments.

Parallax—The angle of difference that an observer sees when he looks at an object from two different positions.

Parsec—The distance from the Earth that gives one second of arc parallax across the diameter of Earth's orbit. One parsec is a distance of 3.26 light years, or about 18 trillion miles.

Planetarium—A closed room with an inside dome for projecting stars and planets in a realistic manner.

Pogson Scale—A standard scale used to determine magnitude.

Polaris—The point star at which the Earth seems to spin. Polaris is a variable star.

Pollux—One of the Gemini Twins.

Prism—A glass shape that is capable of breaking light up into its spectrum.

Process Skills of Science—The skills that a scientist uses when doing scientific research.

Radiation—Either photons or light energy or particles of matter. Radiation can come from the nuclear reaction of the sun, stars, and even objects on Earth.

Rectangular Coordinates—A system of locating an object on a flat surface, such as a road map.

Refractor—A telescope lens that bends light to a precise point called the focal point. A refractor differs from a reflector, which uses a mirror.

Relative Motion—The motion of an object that is relative to the position of some other object. For example, you and I are standing on Earth, which is rotating at about 1,000 mi/hr, yet we are stationary to its surface.

Rigel—The second brightest star in the constellation Orion. This is the beta star in the constellation Orion.

Right Ascension—A coordinate system for measuring east–west on the celestial sphere.

Sagittarius—Found in the southern hemisphere. The center of the galaxy lies behind it. Astronomers pay much attention to this area of the sky.

Schmidt Telescope—A very special telescope with a correcting plate for wide area viewing. It is useful for photographing large areas of the sky.

Sirius (Dog Star)—The brightest star in the sky (minus one magnitude) found just off the right leg of Orion.

Signs of the Zodiac—A band of twelve constellations throughout the sky, centered on the ecliptic.

Solar Prominences—Violent solar storms that eject bright material to great heights above the sun's surface. Some are associated with flares.

South Celestial Pole—A point on the celestial sphere, corresponding to the South Pole of the earth.

Spectroanalysis—Using the spectrum to analyze matter such as stars, chemicals, etc.. This technique is used extensively in scientific use.

Spectra—The band of colors that is formed when a beam of light is passed through a prism or diffraction grating.

Spectral Lines—Dark or bright lines that are formed in the spectrum due to the presence or absence of certain chemical elements.

Spectrograph—An instrument for photographing the spectrum.

Spherical Coordinates—A System of location markers on a spherical surface.

Star Clusters—A large group of stars in a small area.

Star Locator—An instrument designed to help locate the position of stars and constellations at various times of the year.

Star Map—A map that shows where all known stars above a given brightness are in a particular sector of the sky.

Sun Spots—Cooler spots on the sun's surface that appear black. They increase on the sun in an eleven-year cycle.

Super Giant—A star of very great size and luminosity.

Tucana, the Toucan—Constellation found near the South Celestial Pole.

Trapezium—A cluster of four stars in the Orion Nebula; they light up the nebula.

Van Allen Belts—Two donut-shaped regions around the earth with highly charged particles trapped in them.

Variable Star—A star whose luminosity (brightness) varies.

White Dwarfs—Stars that are almost burned out and getting very dim. They are almost as small as the earth.

Zenith—The peak or highest point; apex.

Zeta Orionis—The sixth-brightest star in the constellation Orion.

Zeus—The fictional god that placed Pollux in the sky.

Zodiac—A band passing around the celestial sphere along the apparent path on the sun.